I0607553

DRAGULA
A Transgender Tale

by

John Arthur Long

Based on

DRAGULA THE MUSICAL

Script by John Arthur Long & Theodore G. Kastrinos

Music and Lyrics by John Arthur Long, Theodore G.
Kastrinos, and George Kastrinos

DRAGULA A Transgender Tale © 2019 by John Arthur Long

Published by:

Vellum Publishing, Inc.
PO Box 415
Round Top, New York 12473

All rights reserved, which includes the right to reproduce this book or portions thereof in any form whatsoever.

ISBN: 978-1-7340185-0-9

Except for use in any review, the reproduction or utilization of this work in whole or in part in any form by any electronic, mechanical or other means, now known or hereafter invented, including xerography, photocopying, and recording, or in any information storage or retrieval system is forbidden without the permission of the publisher, Vellum Publishing, Inc.

All the characters in this book have no existence outside the imagination of the author and have no relation whatsoever to anyone bearing the same name or names. They are not even distantly inspired by any individual known or unknown to the author, and all incidents are pure invention.

FOR THEATRICAL PRODUCTION RIGHTS TO
DRAGULA THE MUSICAL, A TRANSGENDER TALE
CONTACT: THE CHAIN THEATRE / 312 W. 36TH ST.,
NEW YORK, N.Y.
info@variationstheatregroup.com

*Author's note: DRAGULA, A Transgender Tale, conveys a message that is clearly and uncompromisingly stated by the main character: "Bigotry, the inability to tolerate the differences in others, is one of the great flaws of our society!" Moreover, when presenting entertainment that represents individuals of the LGBTQIA community, I have endeavored to be sensitive to the courage these individuals have shown and empathetic to what they have endured by living in a manner that allows them to be true to themselves.

John Arthur Long

Memories Of Another Day

Sometimes, right in the middle of a musical number, when the loving audience was cheering and applauding, the memories came. Or deep into the night, the muffled, taunting sounds would claw through all the curtains of protection she had wrapped around her over the years. And, in spite of her entertainment cloak of invulnerability she'd worked so hard to build, in spite of everything, she could still hear the horrible cries. The hate-filled insults. And the years would spin away, drawing her back through agonizing barriers of useless defense when she was no more than a helpless little boy.

Alone. So very alone.

"Baby…fag…pussy…scaredy cat…queer…homo…gay boy," the voices hissed when she had inhabited that small boy's body. The cries of bigotry and hate pierced through the years of memory, as horrible and hateful then as now.

And it was during those dreadful moments of memory that she would allow fingers to move above the soft raised mound of newly-developing breast to gently stroke the delicate petals of the orchid.

Thank God for the orchid, with all its wonderful, sensual beauty.

It was during those times she knew beyond all doubt that she had been right to cultivate her own species of the orchid, this ornate regal flower, with its own special power. Only the comfort of the orchid sustained her through the horrid memories. Just as the original orchid had sustained the male child so long ago. The dried orchid, preserved lovingly within the pages of the King James Bible.

Hidden within dark, protective shadows, her tiny slender boy-fingers would open the feather-thin pages of the Bible, and ever so tenderly caress the delicate form of the flower, savoring this one thing left by a mother who had cared so deeply and protectively.

A mother who had been ripped without warning from this Earth when her child needed her so desperately. A mother who was no longer there.

A mother who had understood when the little child told her he could not behave like they said he should. A mother who had hugged the thin little body warmly when the boy said, "If I knew how, don't you think I would?" That wonderful, comforting being whose warm eyes and caring voice had told the boy "there's nothing wrong; you're just misunderstood." The one person in the little child's life who had said that it was all right to be anything or anyone you want to be. The one who believed and confirmed the belief that change was good.

Yes, mother would have understood that this child, now grown, really had no choice.

Others, like sister Rachael, might wonder why her brother Peter had chosen the path of such isolated loneliness. But Mother would have understood why, in order to survive as she knew she must, she had created this wonderful safe cocoon-like haven of entertainment, dominated by that lovely, haunting creature of the night. Yes, Mother would have understood why her little boy had come to live within this protective entertainment lair for any and all who wished to live beyond what "society" considered to be the "norm." Yes, Mother would have understood why, during the dark hours of the night, once within this entertainment lair, mother's now-grown little person, experiencing such swirling, strange delicious sexual changes both within and without, would slip into that exhilarating protective feminine dressing of entertainment armor to become Dragula.

♫ "I can't behave like they say I should. If I knew how don't you think that I would. There's nothing wrong; I'm misunderstood. And I still believe that change is good."

ONE

THE "G" SPOT

Within the closed padded entrance door of The "G" Spot, an exhilarating beat of musical taunting was provided by The Dickey Chicks. The musicians, in skimpy outfits, played off to one side near the lip-shaped center stage behind which was a huge, rainbow-colored flag, the universal symbol of the LGBT movement, that covered the entire back wall of the club.

Pale but seductive Ivory Tease tickled the keys at the piano, a little too much of a thick though smoothly waxed leg revealed beneath a short high-riding mini-skirt that shifted against the piano stool as Miss Ivory Tease played. And behind the drums, her unseen, high-heeled foot pounding out the steady heartbeat that gave the entire atmosphere within the club a moving edge of excitement as the beat mixed with the rise and fall of shrill voices and cascading outbursts of raucous laughter, sat Timbre Lake, one spaghetti strap of her chiffon blouse having fallen off her shoulder, her dark skin glistening from expended energy against the mountain of jewelry and rings she wore, her large Afro wig moving to the beat she created.

However, it wasn't just the sound of the beat-driven music that captivated the senses of those within The "G" Spot. The very air within the cabaret was a veritable Saks Fifth Avenue perfume counter of scents, wafting not only from small pumps secreted within the padded red leather walls of the club, but also from the oh, so stylishly clothed bodies that filled the dimly lit room. Bodies that not only thrilled the olfactory nerves, but bodies that also offered a feast for the eyes, for these beings were dressed to the nines in finery. Tight, shimmering dresses clung

4

to waxed and perfumed bodies that stood on a collection of stunning high heeled pumps, clogs, and sandals that would have caused a shoe fetishist to weep with tears of envy. Tuxedos outfits, fitted snug around the crotch and over the perfectly toned bodies adorned other patrons, some with the finish of period spats on glistening, shiny black-pointed shoes. And so many, many others, dressed in outrageous outfits, some covering everything, some covering almost nothing. Outlandish outer garments that announced their defiant, declaration of choice, adornments of every style both sexual and asexual that proudly announced, "This is who and what I am. And I'm here to have one hell of a good time. Fuckin' deal with it!"

Oh, how the patrons loved these nights at The "G" Spot. Nights where they could truly be themselves as they sat on the cushioned, heart-shaped chairs around oval tables, each with a phallus-shaped candle at its center, their immaculately nailed fingers holding the stems of breast-shaped glasses that they lifted eagerly to their glossy collagen-filled lips, sipping on colorful umbrella-topped drinks with names like Full Climax, Engorged Cocktail, and the house favorite, Multiple Orgasm. Laughing and drinking, here you were free to be who you really were beyond the glare of the all-too-quick-to-judge society. And, at the same time, to be entertained by the likes of Electra Fying, Downy Soft, April Morning, and Cha Cha Boom, some of the best song-and-dance performers to be found anywhere, some female, some male, some both, some neither, and all created by the center piece of all the magnificent entertainment: Dragula! She was hilarious with her humor, and laughed with you, not at you. And she could both sing and dance like the very best of the Broadway stars. And, unlike so many of the other phonies who only pretended, they knew she truly cared about each and every one of them. Who could ask for anything more? The "G" Spot had it all!

Infield the bouncer sat at his post by the door, alert as always. Each guest in the packed club had passed his inspection upon entry. As always, on the orders of the owner he was absolutely devoted to, Infield had refused no one, but, ever alert, noted any that might prove to be a problem. A lover of the national sports pastime, Infield habitually tossed a baseball or two up and down, sometimes even juggling them expertly as he surveyed the crowded dimly-lit room. Only when he walked was there any sign of weakness in his being, for a slight shuffle betrayed an old on-field injury he had sustained when he was smacked in the groin by a hard hit fly ball. Surgeons gave it their best effort, but were unable to save his crushed "man marbles," as Infield called them. So he had compensated for the impotence of his unfortunate injury by proving his worth, being both congenial to a fault, and always on full alert, all-the-while giving off his casual though confident "I-got-this" vibe. Only his foot-dragging walk hinted at his weakness. And the somewhat strained pitch of his vocal quality, of course. Although, at The "G" Spot, where so many proudly displayed their own "individuality," no one said a word about his slightly distorted voice, which was just one of the many reasons why he loved his job.

Though the club was packed, Infield sat relaxed on his stool by the entrance. Only one couple who passed through the door tonight had set off his bouncer's warning radar. However, so far the two of them, a rather pompous-looking male and his blond female companion, were sitting quietly off to the right. But Infield watched them, nonetheless. Infield watched and saw everything!

As the music from the Dickey Chicks came to a close, the soft lighting in the room darkened, and Infield caught his tossed baseballs in mid-descent, clutching them within his hands. It was show time! Infield loved show time!

Then a single, hot lavender spotlight ignited front and center on the stage. Above the raised platform, a neon sign like the one at the entrance to the club, with its huge pair of puffed-out glossy female lips, appeared. Hurriedly, those who had been standing or dancing found their padded leather seats, put in a second round of orders for Multiple Orgasms, and settled in to enjoy the evening's entertainment. As the noise level continued to drop in volume to no more than a low rumble, Renarde, the emcee of The "G" Spot, suddenly stepped into the center of the spotlight with a flourish of movement and a bow.

"Hello, Darhlings," the emcee crooned softly with a heavy unapologetic faux French accent into the microphone he held suggestively before him. "Uuummmm. So happy to see you. You look good enough to eat. Or at least nibble on a little. Hummmm?"

Renarde was, in a word, outrageous. At close to six feet in height with a medium build, the "G" Spot emcee was dressed in Black and White wide-legged lounging pants, topped with a red long-sleeved tunic. His short, bleach blond hair was shaved in somewhat of a buzz cut on the sides and contrasted sharply with the heavy makeup on his round jovial face, where huge oval lavender-tinted eye glasses magnified his dancing eyes. Someone good at guessing age would probably have put him somewhere in his fifties, but Renarde had a youngish quality to him and, overall, looked very well, if not surgically, preserved. His strongest trait, however, was the personal magnetism that seemed to ooze from every pore of his being. With his flamboyant gestures, dress, and French accent, you simply could not take your eyes off of him. And that was clearly exactly the way he wanted it.

"Renarde welcomes all of you to The 'G' Spot where it is oh, so, HOT, HOT, HOT. Ahhhh,…Renarde sees some of you beautiful creatures out there are first-timers. Don't be nervous. It won't hurt a bit, sweeties. Especially after you have one of our famous drinks, including the house favorite, the Multiple Orgasm. Trust me, if you don't feel good after a Multiple Orgasm, you'll never never feel good. So erase your doubts! All, and I mean ALL: L..G..B..T..Q..I..A and whatever else, ALL are welcome at The 'G' Spot. This inner sanctum of entertainment has been created just for you! A special place where, for a few carefree hours of joyful music, dance, and fun-filled, raucous good times, you are free! So, never fear! You are right where you belong! Aren't they, darlings?" The emcee suddenly stopped, freezing with a gasping intake of breath.

"Oh, but wait. Renarde is suddenly saddened. Do his mascara-laden eyes spy a regular sweetie out there who is ill? The mumps, perhaps?" He squinted out into the audience and then sighed with relief. "Oh, no. Renarde's mistake. It was only a swollen member!"

Miss Timbre Lake hit a rim shot to accent Renarde's joke, and patrons throughout the club chuckled appreciatively. The evening had only just begun, but several were already giddy from Multiple Orgasms. Amid the laughter, Renarde swished down the stage steps and began to cruise among the tables, the spotlight following him.

"So, Darhlings, welcome to you all. You look delicious. And for newies and regulars alike, Renarde wants to remind each and every one of you why at The 'G' Spot, where it is oh, so hot, hot, hot, you can always feel at home because,…."

John Arthur Long

It was here, as always, that Renarde broke into song, rhyming a cute little ditty of his own invention, each time using new lyrics he created on the spot to the delight of both Infield and the regulars. And his pseudo French-accented baritone voice sang out with simmering sensuality.

"♫When you visit The 'G' Spot…where the atmosphere is hot…It's all right to be a…."

Suddenly the emcee stopped. With a frightened look, he glanced around him, bending with a hushed whisper to those who suppressed giggles.

"Wait. Did you feel that? Is it possible? A slight chill in the air at The 'G' Spot where it is oh, so hot, hot, hot? No, it cannot be. Perhaps it was only Renarde's silly imagination."

Renarde pirouetted around an adjacent table with a singing grin and an outstretched flip of his hand. And, as the flamboyant "G" Spot emcee sang, the stage began to slowly fill with low slithering mists of fog, the lighting becoming low and eerie.

"♫When your panic meter fails…Put some polish on those nails, it's all right to be a…."

Renarde suddenly stopped again, this time huddling among the patrons with an audible gasp of fear. At the club entrance, Infield squeezed the balls in his hand even tighter, grinning with anticipation. It was time for his favorite part of the show.

TWO

DRAGULA

Renard gasped once more, his voice trembling in fright as he cowered on the lap of the nearby drag queen and sang:

"♫What is that chill?

I know it's real. It gives me such a fright.

It makes me fear, there's something here

that comes to life at night.

When there's a moon that makes you swoon;

you can't escape its clutch.

What can it be, a he or she;

it wants you oh so much….

They call her Dragula, that haunting creature of the night.

Watch out for Dragula, for you will whet her appetite.

It will be Dragula who makes your heart pound at the sight.

Watch out for Dragula.

She is the Devil's transvestite!

And though you may not fear the presence,

that woos and shimmers in your sight.

It knows your every flaw and weakness. To it, you are the

perfect…bite!

It will be…DRAGULA…who makes your heart pound at the sight.

Watch out for…DRAGULA. She is the devil's transvestite!"

While the words of Renarde's song floated across the room on the vibrato intonations of his rich baritone voice as the emcee sang and tiptoed mysteriously among the smiling patrons, at the back of the anonymously lit stage, a shadowy feminine being materialized from within the fog. The advancing female figure was stunningly attractive and dressed all in red from the top of her flowing high-collared cape and body-hugging dress down to her glistening red high-heeled leather pumps, her wavy black hair framing the small, delicate features of a strikingly beautiful face, accented with hot red lipstick and blazing blue eyes. Pinned to the upper left side of the mysterious being's dress, just above the swell of her left breast, was a fresh purple orchid corsage.

Suddenly, the lights ignited the stage once more in a blaze of color to reveal a sensuously attractive chorus with Dragula at the center. The audience burst into wild applause as Renarde skipped with delight up the steps to the stage, joining the chorus in song, as Dragula, oozing sexuality, began to sing:

♫Sometimes I'm here, sometimes I'm there, sometimes I'm everywhere....

Looking for you, and you and you with something we can share.

Somewhere you'll see me shimmer there in shadows of the night.

The gift that I have waiting, dear, will make your soul take flight.

They call me DRAGULA, that haunting creature of the night.

If I should come for you, I'll make you feel it's oh, so, right."

At this point in the production number, the music slowed to a hot, syncopated rhythm and Dragula, Renarde, and the transvestite chorus danced to the emotion-filled snap and beat of a passionate tango.

Although Infield loved the tango section of the number, he was no longer watching. Movement on the far right side of the club had caught his attention, and he nodded to himself knowingly as the couple he had spotted earlier rose from their seats. The male complained noisily with irritation as he grasped the blond woman's arm and moved among the tables toward the entrance.

"Is anything wrong?" Infield's thin voice questioned as the couple reached him.

"Everything," the male spat at him. "But don't you worry. It will be fixed. You can count on it!" And with that, the man hurried the woman next to him past the bouncer and out through the door of the club.

On stage, the musical number ended to a standing ovation from the crowd, and the performers moved off the stage to mingle and chat among the patrons. Infield looked around quickly, hurriedly shuffling over to where Renarde stood accepting praise from admirers at a table near the front of the stage.

"Yes, what is it, Inny?" the emcee asked, clearly irritated with the interruption. He turned to those around him. "This is Infield, our doorman. His name is actually Ken Field, but he's so fond of the baseball, we've given him his cute little nickname."

Squeezing the baseball in his hand anxiously, Infield nodded to the patrons and apologetically pulled Renarde by the sleeve of his tunic away from his admirers, insisting on privacy.

"There's a fly in the ointment," he whispered to Renarde in hushed secrecy as he squeezed his baseball even harder. "There's something in the soup. There's a customer who spies on us who's not part of the group."

Renarde rolled his eyes. "Please, I'm not in the mood for your secret little rhyme code talk tonight? What is it?" Infield rolled his own eyes with a negative shake of his head, jerking it toward the nearby patrons. "Inny, they're too involved in themselves to care about anything else. Now trust me. Now talk to me. My public is waiting."

"I told you, Renarde. There's a customer who's spying on us not part of the group. He just went out the door. And I really really fear, in some secret way, he'll do harm to The 'G' Spot."

"Inny, Inny. You're wonderful, darhling, and you do a terrific job, but sometimes I think you've been hit by too many fly balls."

"No, Renarde. Listen. He's trouble. I know it."

"Why. Did he do anything except leave?"

"No, but...."

"There, you see."

"But...."

"No more buts, Inny. You're really a dear, but all these butts are giving poor Renarde a hemorrhoid. Now, please. Stop being such a pain is the ass. Renarde's public needs him."

Without another word, Renarde turned from the bouncer to his admirers, and the rejected Infield crossed back through the club.

"What's wrong, Inny? Why the sad face?"

Recognizing the seductive voice that spoke as it came up behind him, Inny turned to face Dragula.

"No one believes me, as usual," Infield responded quietly.

"Oh, I don't know about that. Try me," Dragula replied, wrapping a comforting arm around the bouncer's shoulders.

Infield smiled at Dragula appreciatively and twisted the ball in his grasp as he looked around furtively. "There's a fly in the ointment."

"Oh, is that so," Dragula replied, arching an eyebrow.

"Yes, there's something in the soup. There's a customer who spies on us who's not part of the group. Renarde thinks I'm being paranoid, but I know I'm not. And I really, really fear in some private, secret way, he'll do harm to The 'G' Spot. What do you think?"

"Hmmmm," Dragula answered with a knowing smile. "I think I might just take a look outside and see if there are any unhappy patrons lurking about,"

Infield looked at Dragula with an appreciative smile. "Then you do believe me?"

Dragula hugged the bouncer affectionately. "Let's just say I believe in knowing exactly what's going on, Inny. You know, find out what is true and what is not before things have a chance to get out of hand."

"Right. 'Cause then it would get too hot. And we don't like it when things get too hot, right?"

With bedroom-lidded eyes, Dragula flipped a corner of her blood-red cape back over her shoulder, removed the orchid from where it was pinned onto her dress, inhaling its odor deeply. She smiled with a taunting sexuality, her tongue slowly licking over her full red lips until they glistened with wetness.

"Well, sometimes," she said with a whispered smile.

THREE

No More Intercourse for the Right Reverend Bobby Swagger

Outside The "G" Spot, a fuming Reverend Bobby Swagger stared contemptuously up at the moving lips of the club's sign. Beside him, his assistant, the blond-haired very-well-put-together Miss Tammy Twingle tried to think of what to say to ease the grip of temper that had so firm a hold on her employer.

"You see, don't you, Miss Twingle," Swagger raged, pacing in front of the club entrance as he watched the gigantic lips above him contract and open again. "This is why I followed the calling to come here from my tiny parish at Intercourse, Pennsylvania. I loved Intercourse and I loved the ways of Intercourse. But I knew when the Baptist Ministry informed me I must transfer and assigned me to bring God's word to this den of iniquity, the Lord had helped me realize I had been sent a higher calling. Oh, yes, Miss Twingle. I had my doubts. At first, I did not understand why I could have no more Intercourse. But now I see that my unwavering faith and trust has shown me the way. This is why I have come to live in this Sodom and Gomorrah. This is why I spent all those lonely months at the YMCA among the village people, longing for Intercourse until I was finally able to establish a new humble parish a few blocks from here at the edge of Satan's very back yard. This is my purpose."

Though a devoted employee, Miss Twingle frequently had trouble grasping Reverend Swagger's specific references. This was one of those times.

"Why, Reverend Swagger, you're so strong and courageous. I can't help but admire what you're saying, but I'm not sure I understand exactly what you mean."

Swagger ran a frustrated hand through the locks of his wavy, black hair and pointed to the club entrance. "Oh, my dear, devoted, sweet, naïve Miss Twingle. What did you see going on in there tonight?"

"Well, they all seemed to be having a good time. I think they were genuinely enjoying themselves."

Swagger shook his head, knowingly. "Yes, it's just as I suspected. That's why I brought you along, Miss Twingle. But don't you worry your pretty little head about it. I'll do the thinking for both of us. Because, like you, the naïve have no idea. And that's why it's so dangerous."

"Why whatever do you mean?"

"The spreading sin of subverted sexuality, Miss Twingle!" Swagger snarled, leaning in close to Tammy's face as he jabbed an angry finger toward the entrance in front of him. "This is it! The 'G' Spot is the very core of hedonism. How could you not see the depravity in there? Why, there was every type of LBJ imaginable!"

"I believe…from my research, the initials are LGBT," Tammy corrected, hesitatingly.

"Irregardless, Miss Twingle," Reverend Swagger boomed irritably, "they are the initials of the damned! Because it's like a plague, Miss Twingle, and if it is not stopped, it will grow and spread until it engulfs us all. But that's not going to happen! Because I'm going to stop it. NOW I SEE THE WAY!"

Miss Twingle's head tilted to one side. "How?"

Swagger was moving again now, his steps bold and defiant as he paced. "Not how, Miss Twingle,…WHO! At last I see WHO! WHO IT IS I MUST STOP FROM SPREADING THIS DEGRADATION!"

"Who?" Miss Twingle questioned, her blond hair bouncing as her head tilted in the opposite direction.

"Why Satan's servant, Miss Twingle. Don't you see? This is my mission! This is what took me from no more Intercourse to The 'G' Spot. This is my calling. IT IS DRAGULA! I MUST STOP DRAGULA! That is what will turn the tide. You saw how they looked at Dragula. Clearly, she is the symbol, the representative, the ambassador! Her 'G' spot is the hot pulsating core, if you will, of all this abnormality that is spreading so rapidly here. But how? That's the question. How?"

Tammy's hand went in the air, propelled by an idea that had come to Swagger's assistant as she listened. "Oh, oh...Reverend Swagger, I think I know someone who may be able to help."

Ever suspicious, Swagger frowned doubtfully. "Who? Can he be trusted?"

"Well, he runs a New Age Health Establishment not far from here, so I would certainly think so. The sign reads, 'HEALTH JUICES OUR SPECIALTY. Bringing Good Things to Both Body and SOUL'," Tammy answered with assurance.

"New Age is not New Testament, Miss Twingle! I just don't know."

"But as you always say, 'The old time religion is not old-fashioned. It's as modern as the New Testament is today.' Well, we live in today, and today is new, like the New Testament, right? So, if we can't trust New Age people, who can we trust?"

17

Swagger nodded slowly. "Hummmm, I...think..I see what you mean...."

"The owner name is Cousin Juicy. And his assistant, Miss Tailgate, is so nice too and so talented. " Tammy said, hurrying on, "She can read palms and tell fortunes and everything. And she always gives me a free calorie-reduced but still sweet-tasting Energy Juice drink whenever I'm there. AND...they have these three herbalists who create fantastic herbal formulas for their juice drinks that Cousin Juicy says can cure anything. You just have to tell them the problem and they can mix a formula to fix it. And they're so cute the way they're always arguing as they mix things. Cousin Juicy calls them the Three Bitches...isn't that just too funny?

"I mean, and this is just a thought, but maybe...the problem is merely one of chemical imbalance that a special formula can fix. For example, I probably shouldn't tell you this, but sometimes I have powerfully tempting sensual thoughts when I have too much sugar in my system."

Swagger's pacing paused, and he gave Tammy a thoughtful look, his gaze slipping quickly over her body before he could catch himself and prevent it.

"Well, I doubt if this is a chemical imbalance problem, but one never knows. The Devil works in strange ways. Anything is worth a try. What's this fellow's name again?"

"Cousin Juicy," Tammy repeated, overjoyed that she might have made a helpful suggestion. "And he really does treat you like family, providing all these fantastic juice drinks specifically designed for your personal biological needs. Why I tried the fava bean curd mixture the Bitches prepared for me, and, as you can see, it has kept my complexion clear and my skin baby soft. Just feel me."

Before he could protest, Tammy took a determined step forward, and grabbed Swagger's hand, pulling it slowly over her cheek and neck, the edge of her body touching his.

"Aren't I soft?" She asked.

"Hummm. Yes. Certainly softer than I am at the moment," Swagger admitted, his hand moving in a light caress over the lower part of Tammy's neck to just short of touching her bosom. "I think I'd like to hear some of those sensual sugar thoughts of yours sometime, Miss Twingle. Perhaps I could help with a little…counseling."

"Sure, that'd be swell," Tammy said, her eyes meeting his. "Cousin Juicy has also provided me with a wonderful herbal mixture that the Bitches concocted that has done wonders for a stubborn constipation problem. Five minutes after I down that juicy, I'm looking for the nearest bathroom."

Swagger frowned and pulled back his hand, recovering from the moment's temptation. "More than I needed to know, Miss Twingle. But if this Cousin Juicy is as good as you say he is, we'll see him at once. Because there is one thing of which I am certain: I will put a stop to this abomination!"

The Reverend glared up at the blinking lips above The "G" Spot entrance, and squared his shoulders, his look hard and determined as a confident smile spread across his face. " Why,… I can even out sing those Sin City entertainers! Because my vocal cords are filled by the strength of the Lord!" And with that, his chest swelling with pride, the Right Reverend Bobby Swagger lifted his head, singing proudly to the heavens above the glittering New York skyline:

♫ "I MUST STOP DRAGULA,

THOUGH IT MAY FILL MY SOUL WITH DREAD!

19

I WILL STOP DRAGULA
YES, I WILL MEET HER HEAD TO HEAD!"

As Swagger finished, grinning in self-satisfaction, Dragula suddenly emerged from within the enclosure of the entrance to The 'G' Spot, stepping into the light. With a double-take, Swagger backed quickly away from the overhead awning to stand beside his assistant.

"Excuse me," Dragula said softly, her tone sensual, but filled with concern, "I'm the owner the club, and I don't want my customers to leave unhappy. My doorman indicated you were displeased."

"Not at all," Swagger replied, his entire demeanor changing to one of silver-tongued charm and assurance. "How nice to meet you, Miss...Dragula. I'm sure you understand things aren't always what they seem. The show is very entertaining. I simply got a little hot, and came outside to get some air. By the way, I'm Reverend Bobby Swagger and this is my companion, Tammy Twingle."

Dragula nodded pleasantly. "What a relief to hear you say that. I often worry that watching what goes on at The 'G' Spot might offend rather than provide pleasure. And when my doorman became troubled, I thought perhaps...but as you say, things aren't always what they seem. Well, I really should get back inside. Please stop by to join our festivities anytime, and I'll personally welcome you and Miss Twingle as my guests, Reverend Swagger."

"Please, it's a...Bobby," Swagger replied with a smile and a handshake. "And we'll remember your kind invitation, never fear. Until then...."

Taking Tammy's arm, Swagger hurried away as Infield shuffled out of the club entrance to join Dragula.

"Well, was I right? Is that trouble for The 'G' Spot that I see leaving?" Infield asked as they watched the twosome disappear down the sidewalk.

"Well…, Reverend Swagger said they just needed some air. But you're doing a very good job, Inny, and I appreciate your attentiveness. After all, you never know. Perhaps our visitor doesn't really understand the true attractions that have guided him to The 'G' Spot. That is sometimes the case with first time visitors. I have a talent for spotting these things, you know. And I sense there may be some feelings swirling around inside that tightly-wound, muscular, wonderfully-toned God-given body, that may have drawn him to us and are waiting to surface, inner feelings that the Good Reverend Swagger is not quite aware of. He does have quite the nice 'swagger,' don't ya think? And as Reverend Swagger just pointed out to me. Things aren't always exactly what they seem."

Giving Infield an appreciative pat on the shoulder, Dragula turned and headed back through the club entrance. However, Infield remained at the doorway, frowning as he squeezed the baseballs in his hands and stared intently in the direction where Reverend Bobby Swagger and Tammy Twingle had disappeared down the street.

"And sometimes they are," the bouncer said quietly to his balls.

FOUR

SUCKER TIME

Tailgate was not in the best of moods. While working at arranging various sized juice bottles on the counter of the New Age Health Bar, she had just spilled the contents of a loosely-capped bottle and was attempting to clean it up before Cousin Juicy arrived. Her opportunistic, penny-pinching partner, who would do just about anything to make more money, was such a stickler about wasting anything. And he had seemed so excited about some new money-making opportunity when he called earlier so she didn't want seeing the bottle of one of their preciously newly concocted juices for helping to ease acid reflux spilled all over the front counter to get him upset.

Although Tailgate gave off an air of masculinity, there was also an aura of mysticism about the thick-bodied, self-proclaimed lesbian gypsy. She was dressed in her signature outfit of baggy paisley patterned shirt, dark khaki pants, boots, and was wearing one of her gypsy scarves around her head.

Tailgate muttered angrily to herself as she mopped up the spilled contents with a cloth. It was enough to give her acid reflux which she wouldn't be able to ease because the juicy fix had just spilled all over the damned counter. She wondered which bitch had failed to tighten the bottle cap. Yes, they were very good herbalists and she admired them and they certainly kept her entertained. But they also drove her crazy, the loose bottle cap being a prime example of why. Luckily, Tailgate had just given the counter a final swipe when Cousin Juicy suddenly came rushing in through the entrance.

"Tailgate," Cousin Juicy said in an excited voice, his short-framed, skinny body stopping in front of her at the counter. "Where are the Bitches? We're going to need them to make a new formula 'cocktail'."

"The girls are out," Tailgate answered, hurriedly hiding the soaked cloth behind her and tossing it into the trash container under the counter before Juicy could see it. "They're at the Super Hero Costume nerd convention trying to sell that stupid gigantic hermaphrodite puppet they bought at the Aphrodisiac Fair we attended last week."

Cousin Juicy grinned. "Oh, yes. Ma Daddy! That big anatomically correct puppet thing that has both sexes. Amusing, but a very strange puppet indeed. How could you let them buy such a thing? It's such a waste of money!"

"Oh, I tried to stop them, believe me, Juicy. I only finally gave in to stop all the bitching. They just wouldn't shut up about it. 'Oh, it's so unique! We'll make us a fortune off this thing! Cousin Juicy will be so proud of us'…and on and on and on. They may make us a lot of money mixing formulations, but who on Earth is ever going to need a gigantic hermaphrodite puppet called Ma Daddy?"

"Oh, they're only trying to be enterprising like us. I love those bitches."

Tailgate snorted. "Who are you kidding? You just love the way they're always all over you. Anyway, enough about the bitches. What have you found for us? You sounded very excited on the phone."

Before he answered, Tailgate saw Cousin Juicy's glance settle on the counter. "Did something spill here?"

"Yes," Tailgate said with a roll of her eyes. "Speaking of the Bitches you love so much. One of them left the cap loosened on the new acid reflux juice mixture and I spilled it all over the damned counter."

To Tailgate's surprise, Cousin Juicy only hesitated a moment after taking in the news. "Well, let it go. We can't afford to anger them right now. We need them."

"Whoaa! Juicy doesn't get upset about losing one of his juicies! This must be big. Come on, out with it. What have you got for us?"

Cousin Juicy smiled broadly. "You know that sweet young thing, Tammy Twingle, who comes in here?"

"Ohhh, yes," Tailgate replied, with an answering smile of her own. "I'm not about to forget Miss Tammy Twingle with the big…craving for sweet juicies that stir strange, sensual feelings inside her."

"Well, she works for a Reverend Bobby Swagger who is determined to stop the owner of The 'G' Spot club in the village, a transvestite named Dragula. It seems Miss Twingle convinced the Reverend that this poor confused cross-dressing entertainer may have a chemical imbalance problem…and we're going to help 'fix the problem' with a new mixture."

Tailgate's smile widened. "Hmmm. Sounds intriguing."

"I thought you'd like it. And I've already made the first play, so he's not only on the hook, but indebted to us." Cousin Juicy held up a shopping bag he'd brought in with him when he entered. "I lifted one of Dragula's outfits from the club for Swagger."

Tailgate nodded approvingly. "Resourceful. How did you get away with that?"

"I merely pretended I was from the cleaners and walked right out with it. Oh, yes, Tailgate. How many times do I have to tell you? You can count on Cousin Juicy. I'm not sure why Reverend Swagger wants the outfit, but I am sure the hook is in and we're going to take him to the cleaners. That's why we need to keep the Bitches happy. They're going to make a new cocktail mixture that will be so appealing, Swagger won't be able to resist."

Tailgate said nothing for several long seconds, her hand going to her chin as she thought and considered. Then, she nodded.

"Yes,...I believe it will work. We'll use our persuasive talents on this Reverend Swagger. We already have that cute thing Tammy in our corner, and you have him in your debt by getting the Dragula outfit for him. We'll use a little fortune telling. I think one of my séances should do the trick. Then the Bitches convince the Reverend they can make the stuff he needs. Yes, it'll work! In fact, we can make it the usual two-stage operation. The first part with the bitches' formula will reel him in. And then we'll hit him for the big payoff!" Tailgate raised her hand for a high five. "I think you've done it again, Juicy!"

Laughing aloud, Cousin Juicy answered the high five opening with a slap of his hand against Tailgate's. "You can count on Cousin Juicy, Tailgate! Swagger's taken the bait and now we make him bite! It's Sucker Time!"

FIVE

CHOICES

His hair in a hairnet, the magnificent Dragula wig on a mannequin head next to him, Peter sat in his dressing room at the make-up table, staring into the round-bulbed theatrical mirror in front of him at his frail, slightly-built frame and what he sensed were his already minutely changing features as he re-applied his make-up. Beside him on the dressing table was the usual vase of exquisite orchids, the orchid corsage that had been pinned to the Dragula costume leaning against the vase.

"You were very good tonight. Everyone was," a woman's voice said from the dressing room doorway. Peter turned to see his sister standing in the opening, watching him.

Rachael was dressed in a white blouse and navy blue pants suit outfit that could not have been more out of place at a club like The "G" Spot. Of course, she was older than Peter. But, even so, it was no excuse for the way she looked. Poor, conservative Rachael. Yes, of course, he loved her. She was his sister, after all. And there was no way he could ever repay her for all she had done for him after their mother died. Yet, Peter had always known that, for all of her devotion to him, Rachael would never really understand her brother. And that was even before he had made "the decision."

Now, who knew how she would react to what he had done. Which was why he had decided to wait to say anything about his life-changing decision. To wait until the process was complete. Then he would tell her everything. Because then, there would be no more secrets. Then all would have to accept it. Because it would be clear to not only his sister, but to everyone, that finally, he had become what he had always known resided within this being that had brought him so much hurt and torment not only as he was growing up, but also into adulthood.

But not yet. No, not quite yet. He didn't need the questioning and the doubts and the "looks," making this even more difficult than it already was because…there was no turning back now. The process, with all its swirling emotion and physical changes was occurring right now, this very moment and in all the precious moments to come until the transformation was complete. When, finally he wasn't just a talented performer entertaining others in the guise of the smoldering, sensual Dragula. Oh, yes, he would still be Dragula, the being who entertained and offered sanctuary at The "G" Spot for all who needed or wanted it. But now it would be real! No more just a transvestite performer, but real! Because, right now,…at this very moment, Peter was slowly and irrevocably becoming Patricia.

Peter turned back to the mirror, his right pinky applying a deeper shade of eye shadow to his left eyelid.

"Thank you, Rachael. It was good of you to come. It's been a while since you've seen what we've done with the show."

Rachael stepped into the room, uneasy as always, but with an air of determination. "Yes. I think it's even better than it was the last time I saw it. The new variations in the tango that Renarde added to the dance section are riveting. Quite the audience pleaser."

"It's nice of you to say that," Peter said without turning, his eye contact with his sister through the mirror's reflection.

There was a pause until finally Rachael spoke, breaking the silence.

"Will you be home later?

"I'm not sure of my plans. You needn't wait up, though."

Rachael stared for a moment as she nodded knowingly to the casual response. Then, her body language illustrating she had made a decision even before she spoke, she crossed to the dressing table and, with an exasperated sigh, sat down next to her brother.

"Peter. Could we talk?"

Peter's pinky hesitated ever so slightly at the edge of the eyelid. "Of course."

"No, Peter," Rachael said, her hand finding his arm, stopping the make-up application. "I mean really talk."

Peter lowered his arm, giving his sister a sad smile through the mirror. "So now we know why you really came to the show tonight, don't we."

"Peter, you're my brother, yet I swear, sometimes I feel like I'm living with a stranger. It's like, lately, we never talk."

"We're talking now."

"Yes, because I made the effort to come here. You never talk tome, Peter. I don't feel I even really know you anymore."

"Rachael, please," Peter said, turning to her. "It's not like we travel in the same circles. Stop it now. I talk to you. You're making too much of this. I've just been busy. We'll do lunch soon. I promise."

"No, Peter. No. It has to be more than some superficial lunch conversation. Honestly, what do I really know about you, except that you perform here at your club as the resplendent Dragula, and at home, you are obsessed with growing your orchids. That's it. "

"Rachael," Peter protested. "What's the matter with you? What brought all this on, anyway? What you're saying is just not true. I have been honest with you about my lifestyle choices, the club...everything."

"Really? All right, answer me this. Where did you go earlier this year when you disappeared for several weeks? And don't tell me you

28

were with Harry because I saw him here when I came looking for you. And, having no idea where you were either, he just shrugged, clearly disappointed that you hadn't even confided in him. No one knew where you were, Peter. You were just gone."

Peter shifted uncomfortably in the chair as, his expression blank, he stared back at his sister through the mirror's reflection while, within, his mind struggled with indecision.

Because, on the other hand, was this it? Was it time for him to have the heart to heart conversation with Rachael about what was really going on? The answer that came back was a resounding…NO!

"Rachael," Peter said with hard irritation. "What am I, five years old, that I have to tell you my every move? What does it matter?"

"Peter, it matters to me. So go ahead, humor me. Where did you disappear to a few months ago?"

"You're being ridiculous, Rachael. I did three shows today, I have one more to go, and I'm tired. Let's just drop this conversation, all right?"

"So then…there's no answer because you're too tired to talk to me?"

Peter turned from the mirror, met his sister's gaze for a mute moment, and then turned back to the mirror, his pinky applying more eye shadow.

"Why can't you answer me, Peter?" Rachael pleaded. "What's the big secret? Why can't you confide in me? Is it that you've never gotten over losing Mother when you were so young? Or is it because you were the one who found her and not I? Can't you forgive me for not being there? I swear to God, sometimes I think that dried orchid of hers you keep in her Bible means more to you than I do. Well, I've got a big news flash for you, Peter. Mother's not here! And if that's what's been bothering you all these years, it's about time you faced up to it because she didn't raise you. I did. And I...I think I deserve a little credit."

Rachael was crying now, and Peter turned back to his sister, reaching across to her. "What in God's name is the matter with you, Rachael? Honestly, what brought this on? Was it something I said or did?"

"No," Rachael answered, a little too loudly, pulling away from her brother's hand and standing. "That's the point. It's what you don't do. Why can't I make you understand I care about you, and the separation hurts. Why can't you even meet me just halfway? You're so near, and yet so far away. I've tried so hard to be your friend, Peter. But no matter what I say, you always leave me out."

Peter stood and took his sister's hand. "Rachael, it's not what you think. I do appreciate you and everything you've done, but I'm going through some...changes...in my life right now and...."

Movement at the doorway to the dressing room pulled Rachael's attention momentarily from her brother, and she turned to see Harry, a member of the club's ensemble, standing in his dressing gown at the entrance to the room. Harry smiled in at them, a toenail-polished foot lifting in hesitation with a dancer's precision as it rested lightly against the door frame.

"Oh, sorry. Am I interrupting something?"

"I have to go," Rachael said, pulling her hand from Peter's grasp.

"Rachael...."

"I'm sorry, Peter," Rachael replied, wiping at her face as she hurried by the performer at the doorway, embarrassed by Harry's seeing her so openly emotional. "I...I shouldn't have come...."

Peter hurried to the room's entrance as Harry brushed past him to sit at the dressing table. "Rachael...."

"Never be sorry you've come. That's my philosophy," Harry said as he adjusted his hairnet. "What's with her?"

"I don't know," Peter responded, still looking out of the room after his sister. "She's upset, that's all.

Harry shook his head with a verbal "tsk," and settled the female wig over his own dark, short cut hair. "Women! Can't live with them, and can't live without trying to dress like them," he added with a chuckle. "Rachael is so irritating though. I don't know how you put up with her. I certainly wouldn't."

Peter gave Harry a look of irritation as he sat next to him at the dressing table. "Harry, do I have to remind you that this is my sister you're taking about."

"Oh, sorry. Sorry. But seriously. Why do you care so much? I mean, how often does she come to see you perform? This is the first time I've seen her around here in weeks. And then, when she does show up, she gets you all in a twit. If she really cared, wouldn't she…."

"HARRY!

"All right. All right," Harry said, his hands raised defensively. "End of discussion. So…what are you doing after the midnight show?"

Peter shook his head, putting the finishing touches on his own face as he looked around distractedly. "I don't know. I haven't decided. Have you seen my other Dragula outfit anywhere? I could have sworn I left it in here."

Harry smiled a secretive smile. "No, I haven't seen it. But I know what that means. It means you're going out, doesn't it. What is it? Things getting a little dry around The 'G' Spot? Looking for a new act, perhaps?"

31

Peter applied hot, red lipstick and doused himself with perfume from an atomizer before he sighed heavily and replied.

"Harry, have you ever regretted any of this?"

Harry leaned toward the mirror and smacked his lips together after applying liner. "Life is too short for regrets, Peter."

"No, really. Rachael fills me with such doubt about everything. She seems to think that I'm all isolated and never confide or talk to her. Or anyone, for that matter. I don't know. Maybe it's all wrong. Maybe my life, what I've created here is just an act, like our performance here at the club. Maybe I'm not really living."

"Ah ha! So it is about Rachael. Petie, sweetie, your dear sister hasn't got a clue about our lifestyle. Truthfully, the best thing that could have happened to me was meeting you that night in the Village. You helped point me in a new erection, as Renarde would say. I've enjoyed every minute of it. The lifestyle, the performing. I love my life as Harry." The performer beside Peter stood, and with a flourish of movement, removed his dressing gown to reveal a glittering gown. He struck a seductive pose. "And I absolutely adore my life as Harriet. Look what you are giving those adoring patrons out there. They are deliriously happy to have discovered and become a part of The 'G' Spot. And it's all because of you. Now stop being so maudlin." Using their old gesture of affection, Harry leaned forward and patted Peter lightly on the rear end. "The Truth is, I was hoping..maybe..I could see you later tonight. You know…like old times."

Peter frowned, pulling away slightly. "Harry, we've been over all this. The relationship was a roller coaster of ups and downs…mostly downs. So, we're keeping it on a friendship level. Right?"

Harry shook his head. "Yeah,…yeah. I know all about our ups and downs. You know, the truth is…since you brought it up…what you just said is the one thing I agree with your sister about when it comes to you."

"What does that mean?"

"Well, let's face it. Every time we had a fight, it was because you refused to talk about it. Rachael is dead on about that.

"What! I can't believe this. First Rachael and now you," Peter said. Then, after a pause, he sighed. "Look, forget it. Let's just…."

"Ah Ha!" Harry exclaimed with knowing satisfaction. "You see. There it is. The moment there's a chance you might suddenly become vulnerable enough to actually get emotional about something, you shut it down. That's what I'm talking about. So let me ask you this. Where exactly did you disappear to when you took that mysterious vacation a few weeks ago. Rachael's right about that too. Why is it such a big fuckin' secret?"

Peter stood, genuine anger entering his voice as he spoke. "WHAT! YOU WERE STANDING OUTSIDE THE DOORWAY LISTENING TO US? ARE YOU KIDDING ME?"

Harry brought his index finger and thumb together. "Well, maybe I heard just a tinch of what was said. I stopped outside because I didn't want to be rude and interrupt."

"Unbelievable," Peter said, shaking his head as he sat down in disgust. "I thought you of all people were someone I could trust."

"As did I with you, sweetie. But I was wrong, wasn't I. And, let's face it. It all goes back to that mysterious leave of absence you took that Rachael was talking about. When you came back, you were…I don't know…different somehow. Distant. Suddenly not wanting me near you.

What happened? Was it something I did? Or did you meet someone else? If so, you could at least tell me instead of resorting to all this, 'let's just be friends' bullshit."

"The answer to your question…not that I have to tell you a damn thing,…is no, I did not meet someone else! It's far more complicated than that. And in my own way, I am continuing to deal with it. But let me just say this, Harry. I am what I am. And if you don't like the way I am, you know where the entrance to the club is, right? No one is holding you here."

Clearly upset, but refusing to be drawn any further into an argument, Harry leaned down and placed an arm around Peter. "All right. I'm sorry. All right? Let's stop this. I'm sorry I said anything against Rachael, and I didn't mean to upset you. Like I said. I love it here, and I'll be forever grateful that you helped me be a part of it. Look, let me make it up to you. What do say I go with you when you look for some new talent? Two eyes are better than one when searching for just the right insertion into The 'G' Spot. Hmmm?"

In spite of himself, Peter smiled at Harry's humor, and placed a hand on the arm embracing him. "All right. And I sorry too. I'm not sure about tonight, but when I go talent searching, you'll go with me, I promise, all right?"

"Deal!" Harry said, throwing Peter a hand kiss as he sashayed to the door. "Ta ta, Petie, Sweetie. See you on stage."

After a wave to the departing Harriet, Peter gave himself a final once-over in the mirror, and opened the sash, allowing the dressing gown to slide from his body. The striking red Dragula outfit he wore reflected back at him in the mirror and he smiled sensuously, subtle shifts of movement and posture transforming him into a feminine being, realizing that each day, the transformation was getting, easier…more real!

And, yes, of course, deep down, to use an ironic phrase that sort of symbolized exactly what was going on with the mental and physical changes to his being, he knew the angry response to Harry was tinged with guilt. But, again, there was no choice. He simply wasn't ready to expose this ever-changing body to a physical relationship. Rachael was one thing. But he couldn't even begin to imagine Harry's reaction to the physical changes that had taken place "down there." But as with Rachael, he would also tell Harry everything. When he was ready. When he was finally and truly complete, and no longer a troubled he, but a complete she.

With a final deep sigh, Peter crossed to the coat rack, retrieving the long flowing high-collared red cape, which he wrapped around his shoulders. Then, with movements graceful and feminine, he crossed back to the dressing table, sat once more, and picked up the wig, placing it on his head. In the mirror, his refection became completely feminine. Finally, as Dragula, the reflected figure's hand pinned the orchid corsage on just above the swell of the left breast, and taking a single stem of orchids from the vase, Dragula stood, her slim fingers switching off the lights, plunging the room into darkness.

SIX

MEMORIES OF ANOTHER DAY

Sometimes…now…when she was in this turbulent time of emotion and physical transition, and unbearable loneliness tore at her, she would sleep in the orchid room among her exquisite long-stemmed flowered creations of beauty. Gently, ever so gently, she would place her special orchids all over her changing body, shivering at the touch of their delicacy against her naked skin. They were her children, these creations. Fragile, oh so sensitive beings whose curved colorful paper-thin existence was so vulnerable to the shocks of the world, just as she had been as a child. And so she slept among them to show them the one who had nurtured and cared for them was there to protect them, and also to prevent memories from rushing in on her in sleep when her guard was down.

Often it helped, and she would awaken refreshed and alive, her beautiful orchids being the first thing that filled her vision when she opened her eyes. However, when too much time had passed, the insistent memories tugged at the edges of her consciousness, seeking a way in to plant and spread their agonizing seeds of the past. Sometimes, even surrounding herself with the orchids could not stop them, and the memories would come rushing into her sleep to torment her once again. And, as is the case in dreams, the memories did not arrive on the wings of past reality, but rather they ran through the visual circuitry of her sleep in the compact distorted scenario of a frightening nightmare.

In a dream haze of blue shimmering fog, she would see the child standing alone, cringing in humiliation as the horrible taunting voices filled the air, screeching insults at the defenseless boy, insults that pierced through the child's vulnerability to create open wounds of emotional bleeding that nestled into the corners of his consciousness, festering and refusing to heal. And in the far distance, the boy could hear his sister's voice calling to him, offering to help, promising him that together they could get through anything. However, the child shook his head against the pleading of his sister's voice, shutting it out, knowing that, for all of her caring, she could never really understand his torment. And his tear-filled eyes searched with desperation into the blue haze of fog that surrounded him for the one person he knew he could turn to for comfort.

And, suddenly, there she was!

The older woman floated toward him through the haze, a beautiful orchid in her hand as she rushed to comfort the child. Kneeling, she wiped away his tears, and the horrible voices faded to distant echoes, so faint that, though he knew they were still out there waiting to torment him, they suddenly seemed less threatening. And as he slipped into the comforting arms of the woman beside him, he could hardly hear the voices at all.

They exchanged warm smiles of affection, the mother and child, and she showed him the magnificent orchid she held ever so gently in her grasp, and they marveled at its beauty. Then, meeting the gaze of the child's wide, bright blue eyes, and seeing a smile materialize on his innocent face, as though assured that the child was once again calm, the woman rose and moved slowly away from him, reaching out as her body slipped away.

"Nooooo," the boy mouthed in a silent cry, agonizing when no sound came from him so that she could hear his need for her as he leaped to his feet. And he too reached out, his hand clawing at the air as he tried

37

to run after her, but his body was immobile, refusing to obey his internal commands.

After such a brief moment of comfort, the specter of horrible loneliness began to envelope him once more as he helplessly watched the mother figure beyond his reach stop, her expression going blank and her arms going limp. The orchid dropped from her hand, its fragile petals hurt and bruised as they settled on the ground near the woman's feet. Desperate and unable to move, the child cried out to her over and over, his tiny high-pitched voice pleading, but the woman continued to recede into the fog until her image simply disappeared as it was swallowed up by the thick haze of grey.

Then, of course, too late, the child could move, and he ran forward, turning and twisting in all directions, searching yet knowing even as his eyes gazed frantically into the empty haze that the woman was gone. And sinking in sorrow, he grasped the one remaining thing that he was still able to cling to, his mother's damaged orchid.

She would always awaken at this point, her conscious senses snapping into focus by the sounds of hurtful loss that broke from her throat. Slowly she would regain control of herself. Then, riveting every atom of her being on the beauty of the orchids that surrounded her, she would push her sorrow once again into the unknown depths that lay beyond everyday recognition. For she knew that if she could just concentrate on her orchids and the life she had created in the here and now. Then maybe…oh, God, please let it be true!...just maybe the decision to at last become a real woman would finally put an end to the nightmares of memory that seeped through an unguarded opening, rushing in to haunt her dreams. And at last, she would be able to go on to live a life of fulfillment and peace. Oh, God…Please…let it be true….

SEVEN

THE THREE BITCHES

The Three Bitches worked feverishly around the boiling cauldron that sat on a hotplate in the middle of the counter of the New Age Health facility. Around the boiling pot was an array of herbal bottles and formula mixtures that the Bitches considered and dabbled with as they worked. And, concerning the ingredients for the mixture and its proper preparation, they were, as always, bitching.

"I think the burner's too hot," bitched the First Bitch.

"Well, I think the pot must boil," bitched Bitch Two.

"Being such a sweet bitch, I work and make no trouble. Of course, I can't for the life of me understand why you two insist the cauldron must fire, burn, and bubble," cooed the Third.

"Sweet bitch, my ass, you're a mean bitch, first class," replied the First Bitch. "You must have your say, and only do things your way."

"And I suppose that you don't," put in the Second to the First Bitch. "When we say do this, you say you won't."

"Oh, that's not true!" objected the First Bitch, adding ingredients to the mixture.

"What a bitch," said Bitch Two.

"What a bitch is so true," echoed Three. "If this mixture won't work, Tailgate and Juicy will have our sweet little asses. Then what will we Bitches do?"

"That's right," agreed Bitch One. "And remember what Tailgate said. NO BITCHING!"

Bitch Two shook her head. "You're so full of it. She didn't say any such thing."

"She did too," Bitch Three said to Bitch Two. "For a change, maybe you should try listening, bitch."

Hearing her name as she came into the front of the parlor from her office, Tailgate had stopped for a moment to listen to the bitching. Pulling the cigar she was smoking from her mouth, Tailgate shook her head in frustration.

"Girls, quiet," she commanded, hurrying to where the Bitches were working. "Cousin Juicy is bringing us guests, and they'll be here any minute. Is the formula ready?"

"Oh, Cousin Juicy," exclaimed Bitch Three excitedly. "Do I look all right? He always gives me special attention when he comes."

"He does not," objected the First Bitch. "He thinks you're a cow. He likes me and you know it."

"He does not!"

"Does too!"

"You're both wrong," the Second Bitch interrupted. "Cousin Juicy comes for me."

"Does not," bitched Bitch Three.

"Does too," said the Second Bitch.

"Bitch!" retorted the Third Bitch.

"You're the bitch," said Bitch Two.

"She's right," added the First Bitch. "You are a bitch!"

"GIRLS! STOP IT!" Tailgate insisted. "Can't you ever stop bitching? This is important."

"Well, I can," said the First Bitch. "But it wasn't me. It was that other bitch over there."

Bitch Three took a threatening step forward. "You better stop that, you bitch!"

Bitch One matched her with a forward step of her own. "Make me, Bitch!"

"Tailgate," whined the Second Bitch, "can't you make them be quiet and stop bitching? I'm getting a headache. They're such bitches!"

Making a guttural growl of frustration, Tailgate suddenly reached out and grasped the outer two Bitches around their necks with her enormous hands, banging their heads together against the third, causing outcries of pain from all of them.

"I said QUIET!" the fortune teller shouted, her flexed muscles threatening to break through the material of her shirt. "You're getting me angry. And you don't like me when I'm angry, do you?"

The Three Bitches shook their strangulated heads meekly.

"Then are we going to be quiet?"

All three bitches nodded, not uttering a sound.

All right," Tailgate said, releasing them from the stranglehold. "That's better."

"Bitches," the First Bitch muttered in a harsh whisper under her breath to the other two.

Tailgate shook her head with a sigh of recognition and continued.

"Now look, Cousin Juicy has guaranteed this Reverend Swagger that the formula will work. And is prepared to pay handsomely for it. Is it ready?"

"Absolutely!" said Bitch One.

"We may be bitches…," added Bitch Two.

"But we're very good herbalists," concluded Bitch Three.

"Great," Tailgate said, "because you all know how important it is to Cousin Juicy to make money, and we want to keep him happy."

"Don't worry, Tailgate," Bitch One assured her employer, "it'll work. And this mixture is very strong."

"Just a few drops will do it," added Bitch Two.

"And it's odorless, tasteless, and completely undetectable," added Bitch Three.

"Absolutely!" said Bitch One.

"We may be bitches…," added Bitch Two.

"But we're very good herbalists," reiterated Bitch Three.

Tailgate smiled. "I know. Why do you think I put up with all the bitching?"

Suddenly, a familiar voice called from outside the parlor, and the Three Bitches began to primp and fuss about their appearances.

"Hello," the voice called. "Are there any cutest of bitches in there? Cousin Juicy has come to see you cute bitches."

"He's here," Tailgate said with a warning look to the Bitches. "Now remember, I'll do the talking. And what are you not to do if you want your share of the profits?"

At the mention of money, the three miraculously reached an instant accord.

"No bitching!" the Three Bitches said in unison with innocent nods of agreement.

Tailgate smiled. "That's right. But we've got to make sure we convince him he really needs what we've got. And you know what that means." Tailgate pulled up a chair to a small velvet-covered round table in front of the counter on which she placed a crystal ball. "It's séance time!"

"Oh, I love séance time," muttered Bitch One, clapping softly.

"Not as much as I do," retorted Bitch Two.

"I like it better than both of you bitches. Come on; let's set it up."

"Hello," Cousin Juicy's voice called again from just beyond the entrance.

Tailgate sat down quickly before the crystal ball, gesturing frantically to the Bitches. "They're here, and he's stalling to give us time to get ready. Set things up immediately and don't mess this up. Do it exactly as I've told you. It's is supposed to be scary!"

"Hey, you want scary…we'll show you scary," Bitch One answered, the other two nodding in agreement as they hurried beyond Tailgate to the curtain behind the counter. Bitch One grabbed the edge of the curtain, pulling it closed. At the same time, Bitch Two ran to the counter and turned a switch that lowered the general lighting, but intensified the light against the white sheet of curtain material. Tailgate smiled with satisfaction and turned on a switch that made her crystal ball glow with just the right spooky intensity while Bitch Three went to an amplifier at the end of the counter and switched on haunting eerie music as Cousin Juicy gave a final call from outside.

"Here we come, you Bitches. Are you ready for Cousin Juicy?"

"Hurry," Tailgate commanded in a loud whisper. "Get behind the screen and wait for my cues. And remember…."

"We know. No bitching," grinned the bitches.

"By the pricking of my toe," whispered the Third Bitch, tip-toeing toward the curtain. "Here come the suckers with the dough."

"Put a lid on it, Bitch, and let's go," whispered Bitch Two, grabbing Bitch Three's arm and pulling her to the curtain.

Bitch Two peeked out, pulling the curtain back for the other two. "Get back here, Bitches, and let's start the show!"

Bitch Two dropped the curtain after the other two bitches scampered through the opening, and the curtain settled into place just as Cousin Juicy, leading a cautious Reverend Swagger and wide-eyed Tammy Twingle into the shop. As the threesome entered, Tailgate sat trance-like in front of the crystal ball, weaving slightly to the eerie music.

"Hello," Cousin Juicy said, stopping and squinting in the darkened atmosphere. "Anyone here?" Then seeing Tailgate, Juicy suddenly stopped, his arm going out to block Swagger and Tammy's advance. "Ohhhh, it's your lucky day, Reverend."

"Why…I don't get you," Swagger answered, staring at the swaying figure sitting in front of the glowing crystal ball at the table beyond them. "What's going on here? Why…why is it so dark?"

"Séance!" Cousin Juicy whispered excitedly. "Shhhhh. I know you may have your doubts, but take my word for it. Tailgate is very good at this."

"A séance! Really, Cousin Juicy, I don't think…."

"Reverend," Cousin Juicy answered, grabbing Swagger's arm. "Have I steered you wrong yet?"

"Well, no, but…."

"That's right. You can count on Cousin Juicy."

Tailgate's head suddenly turned in their direction, her eyes snapping open.

"Quiet," her voice hissed. "They have come. Come for you, Reverend."

In spite of himself, Swagger stepped tentatively through the darkened interior toward the mysterious seated figure before him. "What's that? Who? Who has come?"

Tammy Twingle crowded up behind the Reverend, her eyes even wider with wonder. "This is scary," she whispered.

"They!" Tailgate's voice insisted. "The apparitions. They come for you. Watch behind me. Watch and see."

Cousin Juicy nodded earnestly to Swagger. "Now, now we learn what to do. You heard Tailgate, Reverend. They come. They come for you."

"This is so scary," Tammy repeated, edging ever closer behind Swagger.

Suddenly, Tailgate's head jerked back toward the crystal ball, her hands hovering around it as she moaned long and loudly. Behind her, shadowy figures, freezing in awkward poses, could be seen through the illuminated curtain of sheet material.

"Seeeee," Tailgate's voice intoned. "Seeee the shadows that appear. Beings that come from far and near. Tell meeee. What do you seeee?"

"I see weird dead people," Tammy said with a frightened innocent whisper.

"Speeeakk, oh Apparition One," Tailgate requested as the illumination flickered between darkness and light. "Speak, why you have come?"

A haunting high-pitched voice suddenly sounded from beyond the curtain. "SWAAAAGGGEEEEER. Beeewaaaare, beeeesaaare the Queen of Sheeee. For she comes…she comes for theeeeee."

"Geeeee," Tammy muttered quietly.

Swagger spoke in airy-voiced wonder, his gaze never leaving the shimmering figures that wavered in the illumination. "Queen of Sheeee? What on Earth?"

"Drag queen, maybe? And The 'G' Spot," Cousin Juicy offered, helpfully. "Just a guess."

"Of course," Swagger said as the apparition vanished. "Queen of Sheee. The 'G' Spot. Good work, Cousin Juicy. Wait. It's gone. Bring it back. I need to know more."

"Do not fear," was Tailgate's response as her body swayed. "You will hear. Seeeee! Apparition Two…comes for you."

"SWAAAAGEEEEEER," a haunting voice suddenly howled as the ghostly figure appeared in the flickering illumination. "Behold in what you must address. Fear not! For none can harm you that wears a dress."

"There, you see," Swagger said to Cousin Juicy, involved in spite of himself as the shadow vanished. "You were right! Nothing that wears a dress can harm me. That can only mean one thing, right? But could it be true?"

Cousin Juicy nodded. "Sounds true to me. It must be true for you."

"Yes," Swagger nodded in agreement. "This is very good. Is there any more?"

"This is so scary," Tammy whispered, grabbing Swagger's arm.

"Get a grip, Miss Twingle," he said commanded, pulling his arm from Tammy's grasp. "This is important!"

"A THIRD TIME AN APPARITION COMES FROM GHOSTLY SHORE," Tailgate's voice intoned, pulling all of their gazes back to her and the flickering apparition that appeared on the curtain behind her. "LISTEN! It will speak once, and then no more!"

"BEEEEEWWWAAAAARRREEE, SWAAAGGEEEEER!" the swaying apparition's voice howled. "A WARNING COMES ANEW! There'll be no harm 'till wood comes to you!"

"TILL WOOD COMES TO ME!" Swagger repeated as the apparitions vanished amid the flickering illumination. "What does that even mean, Cousin Juicy?"

"You got me," Cousin Juicy shrugged. "The wood thing is a hard one."

Swagger turned to his assistant. "Tammy?"

"I…I'm just not sure," Tammy responded, backing away. "Dead people are really scary."

"I said to get a grip, Miss Twingle," Swagger commanded. "There is no reason to be frightened. We have GOD on our side. And as I told you before, He works in strange ways. This must be something I'm meant to know. But what should I do? That's the question. I must ask. I must speak to them."

As his assistant shook her head doubtfully, chest held high, Swagger turned with bold conviction toward the flickering illumination.

"THIS IS SWAGGER SPEAKING TO YOU! I AM NOT AFRAID! ALMIGHTY GOD PROTECTS ME. TALK TO ME. I COMMAND YOU! TELL ME WHAT TO DO!"

Shadows shifted in the illuminations and indistinct whispering voices could be heard. Then, suddenly, the lights in the interior where they all stood came on, the crystal ball went blank, the music stopped, and Tailgate snapped out of her trance.

She sighed heavily, shaking off the trance.

"That's all," she stated, matter-of-factly. "It's gone."

"WHAT?" uttered Swagger. "What do you mean, 'It's gone?' You have to get it back! I need to know!"

"I'm sorry," Tailgate, said, with a shake of her head as she stood. "It doesn't work that way."

Swagger looked around questioningly. "It all seems so hard to believe now that lights are on. Could it have been real?"

"Ah, there are more things in heaven and Earth, evangelo, than are dreamt of in your sermonology," Tailgate answered, moving to the counter. "What you need to do is make a decision. Juicy mentioned you were interested in a new formula?"

"Ah, yes, the formula," Swagger said, brightening to the reason for his visit. "Miss Twingle assured me the formula in these juices are quite something."

"Of course," Tailgate replied, as she called down the back hallway. "Let me get our herbalists who have been working feverishly on the new formula. Ladies, Reverend Swagger is here!" Then, smiling, Tailgate took Miss Twingle's hand. "Of course, we know Tammy's been quite pleased with our products. How are you feeling, Tammy? Need a sweet lift from one of your favorites of Cousin Juicy's selections?"

"Maybe later, Miss Tailgate."

"Now, Tammy," Tailgate interrupted, giving Tammy's hand a squeeze, "I've told you before. Drop the 'Miss!' It's just Tailgate, to you and anyone else who wants to party."

"Of course…Tailgate," Tammy said. "But right now we need to help Reverend Swagger."

"Actually," Swagger said, after a quick acknowledgement to the three Bitches who suddenly came hurrying into the interior from the back hallway, nodding "hello," and gathering around the cauldron on the counter, "before we get to the formula, I believe I paid you to acquire something for me, Cousin Juicy."

"Ah, yes," Cousin Juicy replied, reaching under the counter and bringing a shopping bag into view. "As I said, you can count on Cousin Juicy. "

49

"Excellent," Swagger said, accepting the shopping bag. "And do you have a place where Miss Twingle might try on a new outfit?"

"Of course," Tailgate said, motioning to the Bitches. "Ladies, would you draw back the curtain?" Hurrying to comply, the Bitches rushed to the curtain area, pulling it open slightly.

"And would you mind trying on the outfit Cousin Juicy has been able to obtain for us, Miss Twingle?" Swagger asked, handing his assistant the shopping bag.

"Whatever I can do to help, Reverend Swagger," Tammy answered, "I'm sorry I became a little frightened before. But I'm all right now. I'll only be a minute."

"I'm Sure Tammy will look wonderful, no matter what the outfit," Tailgate said as Tammy crossed to where Bitch One held the curtain back for her, and she disappeared with the Bitches as the curtain fell back into place.

Swagger smiled. "I think you'll find this outfit particularly interesting. And now…the formula."

"Oh, yes, And as Cousin Juicy will attest, our products seldom fail. I think you'll be pleased." Tailgate turned and called once again for The Bitches. "Oh, Ladies, could we get the formula for the Reverend?"

The three Bitches came running out from behind the curtain, bumping into each other and muttering bitches as they hurried to the counter, one lifting a ladle from the cauldron, one pouring the liquid into a bottle that another held and a third bitch capped. Then they hurried over and handed the bottle to Swagger.

"Here's your Juicy, Reverend," said Bitch One.

"It's a very potent Juicy," added Bitch Two.

"And has no odor and bad taste. Anyone who tries it will love it," said Bitch Three.

Swagger gazed at the bottle in his hand with an arched eyebrow of doubt as he stared at its contents. "And you guarantee it will do the job that it's intended to do?"

Juicy took the bottle from Swagger, tapping it with assurance. "With this Juicy drink, there will definitely be changes to help what you wish for to come true."

"And the price?" Swagger, questioned.

Tailgate shrugged. "Twenty dollars."

Hearing the price, the Bitches gasped and were instantly ready to bitch, but a raised hand from Tailgate silenced them and, muttering, they withdrew back to the area of the cauldron.

"Seems like quite a bargain, considering," Swagger said, eyeing the bottle. "Why so cheap?"

"Well, we like to oblige," Tailgate said. "Then customers will come back when they're interested in more expensive items. And, Tammy is one of our regulars, after all."

"So, is it a deal?" asked Cousin Juicy. "We are ready now, yes?"

"Not quite,...speaking of Miss Twingle. Are we changed and ready, Miss Twingle?" Swagger called toward the curtain beyond them.

In response to Swagger's voice, her hand lifting the curtain, Tammy stepped into view. She wore a red gown with a flowing cape over her shoulders. On her head was a gorgeous wig. Dressed in her new outfit, Miss Twingle was almost an exact duplicate of the transvestite performer, Dragula.

"Now we're ready," Reverend Bobby Swagger said with a knowing smile.

51

"Stunning!" Tailgate said as she appraised Miss Twinge from head to toe. "Just stunning. And you come back and see us anytime, Reverend Swagger. We're always ready to help. And that includes you, Tammy. Au revoir."

With a bow of acknowledgement as Cousin Juicy placed Tammy's original clothes in the shopping bag, a pleased Swagger offered Tammy his arm and they exited. Cousin Juicy gave Tailgate an approving wink of satisfaction and then hurried after them.

Immediately, the three Bitches came rushing over to Tailgate.

"Tailgate, I've got a bitch. Twenty dollars?" bitched Bitch One.

"Yeah," added Bitch Two. "How can we get rich on twenty dollars?"

"Yeah, we work our fingers to the bone coming up with a formula and you practically give it away? That's a real bitch! What gives, Tailgate," put in Bitch Three.

Tailgate smiled knowingly. "Ah, ah, girls. No bitching. You promised, remember.

"Yeah, but," protested the Bitches.

"No buts!" Tailgate insisted. "Juicy and I know what we're doing. We have seen the future and it is ours. Oh, yes, your formula will tantalize. But only just enough to bring them back to us. And when they come back, desperate for success, they'll be ready to pay anything to acquire the ultimate satisfaction that we convince them only we can provide."

"But, Tailgate. I'm not even sure our formula will work the way these other two were messing around with it," said Bitch One.

Bitch Two gasped. "What do you mean, the way we were messing around. You're the one who kept the fire too hot, bitch."

"No," added Bitch Three. "You two were both the ones who made it burn and double bubble. I wanted to keep a steady temperature, but, noooo."

"Oh, yeah. Listen, you bitch," huffed Bitch One.

"Look whose calling who a bitch…bitch," shot back Bitch Three.

Tailgate shook her head and turned to head down to the back hallway to her office as she muttered, smiling in spite of herself. "They drive me crazy, but they're my bitches."

EIGHT

SNAGULA

Glancing around them as they hurried across the intersection, Cousin Juicy, Reverend Swagger, and a red-outfitted, magnificently wigged Miss Tammy Twingle moved to the center of the block on 13th Street in the West Village.

"Are you sure he'll come this way?" Swagger asked as he shot continual glances over the pedestrians moving toward and away from where they stood.

"Absolutely," Cousin Juicy assured the Reverend. "You can count on Cousin Juicy. I've watched everything, just as you asked, and the doorman's schedule never varies. He always takes a break between shows to get away from the club and stroll around for a while. It's always the same routine. Never fear, Reverend Swagger. This game of 'Snagula' will not fail our first test."

Swagger smiled. "Snagula! Very good, Cousin Juicy. I like that. Excellent. And are you ready, Miss Twingle?"

Tammy nodded to Swagger, but bit anxiously on her lip. "Yes, but, Reverend Swagger, I…."

"But what, Miss Twingle," Swagger protested, stepping back slightly and admiring his assistant. "Look at you. You're perfect."

"Oh, I know the look is there. I saw my reflection in the stores' windows as we came down the street. But, Reverend, it's the talking I'm worried about. Lord knows, I'd do anything to help the cause, but this…I…I'm just not sure I can be convincing. I mean, I'm not an actress. I can't act."

Swagger took Miss Twingle by both her cape-laden shoulders and gave her a little shake of assurance. "Of course you can. There's nothing to it. A different gesture, a change of voice. Acting is easy. You just have to pretend. Tell her, Cousin Juicy."

"Oh, yes, Miss Tammy. The Reverend is right," Cousin Juicy said with reassurance. "You can do it. There's nothing to it. I've watched these actors many, many times. What do they do? They don a wig and take on an alter ego. It's easy to be an actor. You simply just pose. You scream and shout, never showing the slightest doubt, and nobody ever knows."

"Exactly," Swagger continued. "It's easy to be an actor, Miss Twingle. You just need to have faith. We've made the plan, and you can do it. I know you can. You change your voice and switched your clothes, and nobody ever knows."

"Yes, you can do it. No question," Cousin Juicy reiterated.

An unassured Miss Twingle continued to nibble at her glossy red lower lip nervously, however. "I don't know, Reverend. I just...."

"Now, Miss Twingle, you must forget your doubts," Swagger insisted. "The game of Snagula's afoot, and we're going to win. You can do it. A little practice at lowering the voice to match Dragula's intonations, and you're off. Tell you what. Try this phrase in Dragula's voice. Repeat after me: 'Those nags who dress in drag we have to snag.'"

"Those nags who...dress in...drag....we...have...to...shag,"

"No, no. That's snag, not shag, Miss Twingle," Swagger corrected. "What a difference a word makes. Now try it again. A little lower in pitch this time: 'Those nags who dress in drag we have to snag.'"

"Those nags who dress in...drag...we have to...snag," Tammy repeated, a little less tenatively.

"Better," Swagger said, encouragingly. "Again."

Tammy scrunched up her face and pursed her lips with determination. "Those nags who dress in drag we have to snag."

Swagger glanced at Cousin Juicy with the beginnings of a smile. "I think she's got it. Cousin Juicy, I think she's got it. Again...."

"Those nags who dress in drag we have to snag," Tammy repeated, duplicating Dragula's voice and cadence of speech exactly.

"Yes," Swagger said excitedly, breaking into a song of encouragement. "She's got it. By heaven, she's got it! ♫ Now once again, what must we do?"

♫"We must snag...we must snag."

♫ "And who is it that we must snag?"

♫ "THOSE IN DRAG...IN DRAG!" Tammy sang back in delightful confidence.

"YES, MISS TWINGLE, YOU'VE GOT IT!" Unable to contain himself, Swagger gave Tammy a big hug of his own, pressing against her as he held her in his arms a tad longer than necessary. "You're going to be fantastic! Isn't she, Cousin Juicy?"

"Oh, yes." Cousin Juicy grinned. "No one will ever be knowing in this game of Snagula."

"All right, Miss Twingle," Swagger said, leading Tammy to stand under the glow of a streetlight. "I think you're ready for our first "test" before we commit to the real deal."

"I'm sorry," Tammy said to Swagger with a mischievous smile. "Were you talking to me? I'm afraid I don't know a Miss Twingle."

Absolutely giddy with delight, Swagger gave Tammy one more quick hug when an approaching figure with a shuffling gait caught his attention. "Someone's coming. Oh, it's the club's doorman. You're right, as always, Cousin Juicy. Thank you, Jesus. This a perfect for our test run of Snagula. Now we're going to get out of sight, Miss Twingle,…that is, I mean,…Miss Dragula. But never fear. We'll just be around the corner, watching everything."

"Bye, bye, boys," Tammy said in her Dragula voice, blowing them a kiss as Swagger hustled quickly away down the street with Cousin Juicy hurrying after him.

While Tammy arranged herself by leaning seductively back against the lamppost, Infield approached, muttering excitedly while juggling two baseballs, tossing them into the air and catching them as he shuffled up the sidewalk, oblivious of those giving him a wide berth as they walked around him.

"What a day," Infield exclaimed, fondling and squeezing the balls he held. "I've never been so lucky. Catching two humming flies in one game. Oh, how wonderful it is to feel the texture of the hard baseball as it painfully and forcefully hums into the awaiting flesh of your Venus mound, sending delightful shivers of painful pleasure through you. And today, it didn't just happen once, but twice. That's two hummers in one day! Oh, the joy! There's nothing like it. Unless later, when you can spend some time with your new balls, enjoying the feeling of your balls in your hand."

Concentrating intently on the balls in his hand as he walked and talked, Infield almost collided headlong into a passerby who glared at him angrily. The "G" Spot bouncer uttered an apology, forcing himself to watch where he was walking rather than admiring the balls he held, which is why, looking up, he spotted the red-caped feminine figure leaning against a lamppost up ahead of him.

"Hey," Infield said, smiling in recognition. "That's Peter. Wait till he hears I caught two humming flies at the game. He won't believe it."

As Infield spoke, far ahead, he suddenly caught the flash of a second red outfit approaching the intersection from across the street. Gasping with amazement, he did a double take, glancing first up the block to his right where Dragula leaned against a lamp post, and then to across the street where Dragula had stopped at the street corner two blocks ahead, waiting for the traffic light to change.

Dumbfounded, Infield leaped behind the corner street sign pole, frantically juggling his baseballs in an attempt to hang onto them in his alarmed state.

"Oh my God," Infield gasped, gripping his baseballs tightly as he peeked around the street sign pole, looking first toward where Dragula stood primping under the overhead glow of the streetlight, and then to where Dragula waited for the light to change.

"TWO DRAGULAS!" gasped Infield. "Oh my God! This really has my balls in an uproar. There isn't just a fly in the ointment. There's a fly in some deep shit if my eyes don't deceive me."

"Is that you," Tammy-as-Dragula cooed as Infield reached the lamplight.

Infield rolled his eyes, tossing first one ball in the air and then the other. "Oh, hi. I'm not doing nothing. Just playing with my balls, that's all." Infield's ever alert gaze swept over Tammy-as-Dragula as he juggled his balls. "By the way, where's your flower? I don't think I've ever seen you without it before."

Caught off guard, Tammy-as-Dragula turned, stumbling momentarily. "I…I must have forgotten it. Well, I've got to get going…back to the club. 'Til later. Ta ta."

"Ta ta," Infield answered innocently as he watched Tammy-as-Dragula hurry away in the opposite direction and around the corner out of sight. Then, in sudden panic, Infield spoke desperately to the balls as if they were his closest friends.

"Oh, no, what should I do, Balls? Things were so good catching two hummers, but now with two Dragulas, things are so bad." Suddenly the second red-capped figure snagged his attention away from his balls. "Someone's coming. It's Dragula. Oh, but is it really Dragula? How can I know for sure." He looked frantically from one ball to the other, when, suddenly, the answer came to him. "Wait! I know. The flower! I've got it, Balls! Only the real Dragula wears a flower. Don't you see? That's how we'll know what to do since there's two."

"Inny," called Dragula, seeing the anxiously twitching doorman as she approached. "Have you seen Harriet? I promised to take her with me to check out a new prospect for the club. I'm sure she said she'd meet me here."

Not sure what to say, wide-eyed with anxiety, Infield squeezed his balls, carefully eyeing the orchid Dragula was wearing.

Frowning at the mute doorman, Dragula shook her head. "Honestly, Inny. The girls are right. You are so strange sometimes. But, not to worry. I still love you. Now, what's the matter?"

"There's a fly in the ointment. There's something in the soup," Infield insisted. "And I really, really fear that this time it's bad news. 'Cause where there used to be just one, you can now find two of youse."

"What? What is this? Some kind of riddle I'm supposed to figure out?" Dragula said in amazement.

"No!" Infield replied, "You have to listen…."

"Nevermind," Dragula said, seeing Harriet approach and giving her a wave and hurrying off in her direction. "Here's Harriet now. I'll see you later at the club and you can tell me everything. Alright?"

"Alright," Infield answered, turning to go back to the club after watching Dragula and Harriet depart, his attention back to the balls in his hands as he hurried away. "You can count on it. I'll tell you everything. Because things are *not* always what they seem, are they, Balls."

In the meantime, after Tammy rejoined them where he and Reverend Swagger hid out of sight behind the marque of a diner around the corner, Cousin Juicy heaped praise on Tammy, who beamed with pride at his words.

"Did I not tell you you could do it, Tammy? We saw it all. That doorman bought it hook, line and sinker. And if he's fooled, we can waltz right past him and into the club when the time comes."

"Well done, Miss Twingle, I must say," Reverend Swagger added. "An Academy Award performance if I ever saw one." Swagger opened his arms invitingly. "May I be permitted to give a congratulatory hug and kiss?"

Tammy smiled, moving into the Reverend's open arms. "Of course, and please call me Tammy, Reverend Swagger."

"All right...Tammy," Swagger said, taking Miss Twingle into his arms. "And you should call me Bobby."

As Tammy and Swagger went into a prolonged passionate embrace, Cousin Juicy stood awkwardly next to them and, the seconds ticking by, he joked to fill the void.

"Say, Reverend Swagger. The joke is on you, eh?"

"I...I don't get you," Swagger answered distractedly, eyes only for Tammy.

"Well, take a look. It isn't Miss Twingle you're kissing. You're kissing Dragula. And pretty enthusiastically, too, from where I stand. Is that not a funny joke on you?"

Staring at Tammy in Disbelief, Swagger wiped at his lips with the back of his hand, and stepped away from Tammy with a shudder.

"Oh, good lord. Of course, that explains it. That must be the reason."

"Explains what, Bobby?" said a confused Tammy.

"Why I felt no emotion when we kissed. Why I felt no passion. Praise the Lord for always showing me the error of my ways. We must stay ever prayerfully alert. There can be no slippage. Don't you see? Because this is not the time for the temptation of frivolous congratulatory kissing! Just because the doorman was fooled doesn't mean someone as clever as Dragula will be. No, the Lord is tellin' me this must be perfect. So, back to the parish, Miss Twingle. Put your faith in the lord and practice, practice, practice and, God willing, practice will make you perfect!"

Without another word, his gaze of conviction upward to heaven, Reverend Swagger rushed past Tammy and Cousin Juicy and down the street.

"Reverend Swagger," Tammy called in confused dismay. "I mean...Bobby, wait."

NINE

NEVER A CHOICE

"Canuse! Canuse! Canuse!" rang out the shouts from the crowd at the evening political street rally. Complementing the noise of the crowd, a Spanish combo played, bringing even more life and excitement to those gathered in support of their favorite candidate for mayor of the city.

José Canuse, the slightly built though exuberant Hispanic mayoral candidate, stood before the crowd gathered at the corner, his arms raised and his body moving unconsciously to the pulsations of the music as he smiled and nodded appreciatively to his enthusiastic supporters.

Up the street from the chanting multitude, stood a statuesque red-caped feminine figure accompanied by her friend, Harriet.

"Well, I can see José certainly has this crowd in his political pocket," Dragula said as, ever the showgirl, she shifted her position next to Harriet just slightly so that her figure was accentuated by the illumination of the overhead streetlight. "And he doesn't just want this crowd. He wants as many different factions of the city as he can muster in his campaign for mayor. That's why I thought it would be a good idea for us to see him in action before he came to the club."

Harriet gave Dragula a look of amused surprise. "José Canuse, the great champion of the city's minorities, is coming to The 'G' Spot?"

Dragula returned Harriet's look with a smile of her own. "I knew you'd be intrigued. Apparently, he wants to bring his message to and garner the support of the particular minority faction that frequents clubs like ours, so he's booked The 'G' Spot for one night next week. I'm swamped with things to take care so do you think you could be a dear and come up with some appropriate entertainment for mayoral candidate Canuse? Bawdy, but not too bawdy."

The crowd cheered loudly, and José, his body still moving to the music, quieted the supporters with waves of his outstretched hands.

"Oh, I…I think Renarde and I could come up with something interesting," Harriet said.

"Actually, perhaps he should be a part of such entertainment. Hmmm?" Dragula suggested with a mischievous smile as she watched his body move.

"That's not what I had in mind," Harriet responded quickly, grasping Dragula's suggestion. "You've got to be kidding. You're so rash and unpredictable lately."

"Ah, but look at those moves," Dragula said as the mayoral candidate spun around to the pulsations of the music as he wooed the onlookers. "I think he'd be a perfect addition to the entertainment. Who would know but us, and José, of course. Let's see how things go when he pays the club a visit."

Harriet shook her head. "I don't know. I think you're wrong about this one. I can't believe you don't see that." Beyond them, the crowd followed the mayoral candidate as he proceeded down the street toward the park. "Good, he's leaving before you might yield to the temptation of suggesting such a thing to him. Let him go. I swear, you're losing your touch if you think Canusé is right for The 'G' Spot. Something like that could only open up the club to possible jeopardy."

Dragula's face suddenly flushed with anger. "What? Who the hell are you to tell me I'm losing my touch! I built the 'G' Spot from the ground up! How dare you…!"

"All right, damn it!" Harriet answered, with a foot stomp of aggression. "Enough! Let's deal with this. Right now! There really is something going on with you. I don't know what it is, but there's something...off. These outbursts of temper! Not even listening to other opinions the way you used to. We can't even talk anymore. You're just not yourself. And once and for all, I want to know what's going on."

"Paaaleeeease," Dragula said. "Must we keep going over and over this. And this is certainly not the time or the place for some intimate relationship discussion."

"Wrong! There never is any right place or time. And the time is now! I want to know what is going on with you, and I want to know right here and right now. So spill it!"

There was a long pause as the two stared at each other. Then something in the expression of the Dragula face glaring at the Harriet shifted, and the voice that answered was no longer that of Dragula, but Peter.

"All right," Peter's voice said, matter-of-factly. "I...I'm becoming a woman."

"Oh, no," Harriet responded, grinning. "Don't try to sidetrack me with bullshit. Look at you, my dear. Becoming a woman is hardly news."

"No, Harry," Peter answered, using Harriet's real name, determined, now that the truth was finally emerging from within where he had been holding it for so long. "I don't mean the Dragula transvestite entertainment charade. I mean I am becoming a real woman. I started the therapy well over a year ago...and then the drugs,...and...and then, when I took that leave of absence you've been so eager to know about...I had the operation. And the transformation is happening. I can feel it happening, and…."

"WHAT? You can't be serious!" Harriet interrupted loudly, refusing to match Peter's change into the male persona.

"Yes," Peter continued, pushing forward now. Committed. Actually feeling a rush of relief spreading through him. "Yes. It's the truth. I'm in transition and becoming a woman. And I'm sure the transition, both inwardly and outwardly, is probably having a certain effect on my demeanor, and, for that I'm sorry if I…."

"And you didn't," Harriet stammered. "When…when did you plan to tell me?"

"Of course, I planned to tell you," Peter said quietly. "I've just been going through an…adjustment period. But the therapy continues to go well. I just wanted to wait until…."

"What? Until your transgender coming-out party?" the drag queen said with a sneer.

"Try to be a little more understanding. This isn't the easiest…."

"Oh, I understand, all right, you secretive little bitch," Harriet shot back. "You couldn't even discuss this with me, of all people, before making such a monumental decision. Wait!" There was a gasp as a realization hit, and mascara-laden eyes glanced downward. "When you say operation, do you mean…?" Unable to say the words, Harriet looked away in frustration. It was then, her gaze stopped on a figure standing by a light pole on the opposite side of the street, and she shook her head as overwhelming frustration spilled out. "OH, GREAT! PERFECT TIMING! Just what I need. Because unless my eyes deceive me, isn't that your sister Rachael over there?" Harriet raised her cashmere-gloved hand and waved in Rachael's direction, calling to her in a sing-song female voice. "Hiiiii!"

Realizing they had seen her, Rachael hesitated, then looked in both directions to be sure there was no traffic, and hurried across the street to where the two drag queens stood waiting for her.

"Not a word about this to Rachael," Peter said as they watched her approach. "I mean it!"

Harriet said nothing, the toe of her right high-heeled pump tapping angrily against the pavement as she merely stared out at the approaching Rachael.

"Rachael, what are you doing here?" Peter asked as she came to beside them. "Are you spying on me?"

Rachael held her brother's gaze, refusing to lie. "Well, how else am I going to find anything out?"

Peter's eyes widened, surprised that he was correct. "So you are following me? You've got to be kidding."

"And you think sneaking around behind your brother's back is the way to go, Rachael?" Harriet put in, pointing at her accusingly with the nail-polished end of her index finger.

"I really don't see how any of this concerns you," Rachael replied, an edge of anger in her words.

"Would you please just let Rachael and I deal with this," Peter said.

"No, I will not," came the huffy reply. "Frankly, I'm getting a little tired of being silenced every time anything involving your sister comes up. And, this on top of what just happened!"

"All right, look," Rachael said quickly. "I'm sorry. I'm not trying to cause trouble. I just thought I might gain some insight if I learned more about what, where and why…Never mind. I'll just leave."

Peter shook his Dragula-wigged head. "No, Rachael. That is not necessary. Harry didn't mean anything by what he said."

The drag queen's mouth opened in protest. "EXCUUUSSSE ME, but actually, yes I did, Peter! And I think I can speak for myself, if you don't mind. Because I meant exactly what I said. And if you don't see it that way, maybe I'm the one who should leave."

Peter held up his hands. "Would both of you just stop it, please."

"Not the answer I was looking for Peter," Harriet's said, red lips pursing together in anger. Then, after a pause, she continued, hard and determined. "You know what? It's pretty clear you and your sister need some time *alone* to work things out."

"Stop it. Don't be ridiculous."

"Ohhhh, you think I'm being ridiculous? Well then, how about this? I'm sick of this conniving sister of yours always sticking her two cents in where it's not wanted, all right? AND, frankly, I'm devastated that you didn't feel the need to discuss your decision with me, so maybe we should make my departure permanent. I'm not sure I want to date a woman anyway!"

"SO YOU'RE JUST GOING TO WALK AWAY…." Peter called as the drag queen, not turning to Peter's insistent voice, stomped off in an angry huff, high heels clicking against the sidewalk as she hurried away from them.

"Thanks a bunch, Rachael," Peter said to his sister. "Harry and I haven't exactly been hitting it off recently. Can't you just leave well enough alone instead of always trying to reach out to me?"

"Peter, maybe you can't see it, but the only person Harry really cares about is Harry. You heard him. 'I'm not sure I want to date a woman.'

What does that mean? You two have been together almost since he joined the troupe at the club. He's so full of it! And excuse me for trying to break through that impenetrable shell you've created around yourself."

"Well, secretly following me around is certainly not the way to gain my confidence, I can tell you that," Peter said.

"You know what," Rachael replied, clearly embarrassed by her actions and yet unable to suppress an angry response. "I am done! You want to isolate yourself from someone who really cares about you, fine! Enjoy the shallow applause being the drag queen Dragula provides!"

"So, there it is, isn't it!" Peter answered loudly. "You've finally let it come squirming out of you. The truth! What really bothers you about me. And you wonder why I won't confide in you, Rachael, after you say something like that about my being Dragula. Oh, I know you try to hide it. You try to be the nice sweet sister. But it's still there, isn't it. Festering inside you 'till you can't stand it anymore and that's what brings you sneaking around. That's what you really want to talk to me about. THE PREJUDICE AGAINST MY LIFESTYLE! The prejudice that makes you no different from all the rest. That's what really bothers you, isn't it. You want to know why your dear little brother can't just be 'NORMAL' so you don't ever have to be embarrassed because of what he is."

Rachael met her brother's accusing gaze, her own eyes filling with tears, and when she answered quietly, all traces of anger were gone from her voice. "No, you're wrong, Peter. But you don't want to believe that. You're so goddamned defensive about how you've chosen to live, you'd rather turn my caring into something negative because then you're safe, aren't you. If you let no one in, no one can hurt you. Obviously, there's something you haven't told me, or Harry wouldn't have said that thing about your…decision. Right? Okay, fine. If you need me, I'll be there. But I'm through going up against a brick wall. The choice is yours."

Peter started to reply, but was interrupted by one of three rough-looking men who had gathered around them. So intent had they been on what they were discussing, neither had noticed the men who now surrounded them, sneering and laughing.

"Hey, Gay Boy," laughed the man closest to Peter, making kissing noises. "You bothering this lady? How 'bout you just leave, huh?" With a raised hand, the man suddenly shoved Peter. "You heard me! Get the fuck out of here, you and your queer man-dress!"

"I'm not being bothered," Rachael said defensively. "I'm his sister. Leave him alone. He's not harming anyone."

"WRONG!" shouted the second man, shoving Peter back to the first. "He's harming my eyes! You heard my friend. Get the fuck out of here! Go on, before we teach you a lesson and rip that tranny dress the fuck off your faggot little body."

"Please, we don't want any trouble," Peter said, moving away from the two.

The third man suddenly grabbed Peter's arms from behind, stopping him and nodding to the other two. "Then you shouldn't have worn the dress, queer boy. 'Cause it's fucking lesson time!"

Laughing, the first man rushed in, punching Peter in the stomach as the man holding Peter kicked his legs out from under him. As Peter gasped, falling to the pavement, the second man moved forward, kicking savagely at Peter's fallen body. Rachael screamed, attempting to stop them, but the third man grabbed her, holding her back as the other two men pummeled the fallen Peter, who groaned beneath the assault of
punches and kicks.

"HELP," Rachael screamed, struggling against the man who held her. "STOP IT! HELP! SOMEONE HELP US!"

"Quiet down, Gay-boy lover," hissed the man who held her, slapping her across the face. "or we'll teach you a lesson too for hanging out with faggots."

Suddenly a loud whistle blew, and, seeing a policeman rushing in their direction, the man holding Rachael released her, shouting to the other two. "SHIT! IT'S THE POICE! LET'S GET THE...GET THE HELL OUT OF HERE!"

After the first man gave Peter's pain-cradled body a final kick, the three ran hurriedly away, jeering and laughing as the policeman came running up to Rachael and Peter, stopping momentarily to where Rachael bent to comfort her injured brother.

"You all right, here?"

Peter, sitting up with Rachael's assistance, waved the officer off. "I'm okay. Just a little shaken. Thanks for your help, officer."

Looking toward where the men were disappearing, the policeman hesitated. "Well, all right. If you're sure you're okay. I can put an APB out on them if you want to furnish a description and press charges. I didn't get a very good look at them before they bolted."

"No," Peter said, coughing and shaking his head. "I'm sure they're gone. They won't...they won't be back to bother us anymore. And I'll be fine. Just need to catch my breath."

"All right. If you're sure you'll be okay. You see to your friend here," the officer said to Rachael. "I'll just make sure they're gone and not coming back."

"Oh, Peter. Peter," Rachael whispered emotionally, holding and comforting her brother as the policeman hurried away in the direction the men had run. "You sure you're okay? That nothing's broken...?"

Peter shook his head. "Just bruises,...I think. They'll heal." He gave his sister a weak smile. "I guess it was a good thing you were here, after all."

Rachael rocked her brother, stroking him comfortingly as she held him in her arms. "I love you, Peter. But don't you see? This is exactly the kind of thing I worry about. That something horrible will happen to you because of the choices you've made."

With an expression of deep sadness, Peter raised his head and looked up at his sister, his voice cracking with emotion as he spoke. "You...you think the choice is mine? My dear sweet Rachael, you couldn't be more wrong. Oh, Rachael, don't you see? As if I had a choice. As if I ever had a choice...."

TEN

MEMORIES OF YESTERDAY AND
HOPE FOR TOMORROW

There was an unanswered question about "the incident," as she referred to the horrible encounter, that baffled her. After the emotional upheaval and the depression and the physical pain, while she took refuge with her orchids, sleeping with them, feeling their comfort as she nursed her emotional and physical wounds, the nagging unanswered question surfaced, refusing to go away.

Why? Why had this happened now? Why now, when everything was changing for the better, had the demons and nightmarish fears of the past suddenly materialized into reality to confront her? She wrestled with that one unanswered question throughout the night until the exhaustion from lack of sleep finally took her into unconsciousness. Only to awaken to the beauty of her exquisite orchids, those delicate darlings that made it possible to go on, but with no solace from the unanswerable question that tormented her.

And then, lying naked among her many beautiful curl-pedaled darlings as the soft rays on the morning sun poured in through her window, bringing warmth and comfort, the unbidden memory of a fleeting promise came to her. Hanging onto that hope of a promise she'd made to the lovable shuffling being who spoke with a slightly distorted voice in strange rhymes, she managed to pull herself together, get dressed, make it to the club, and talk to Infield.

As the strange rhymes of information came tumbling forth from the sweet bouncer she adored, suddenly new hope took wing, as it all became clear, the doubts that had nagged at her sleepless night washing from her in a receding tide of relief.

Finally, she understood.

Infield, with his silly, lovable insisting rhymes had been right all along. There really was a fly in the ointment, and the demon had a name: Swagger! Through Inny's warning rhymes of double images and disguises, it didn't take very long for her to realize that this devious religious zealot had a plan and, though she didn't understand exactly what was going on, one thing was clear. The objective was to somehow discredit her and The "G" Spot. And in place of the anguish the horrible "incident" had caused her, sweeping in with a newfound fury to fill the vacuum left by the departing emotional torment, came a new resolve: revenge.

For this she knew. Yes, she could be hurt,…had been hurt badly by those prowling racists of hatred. And she could suffer from self-doubt. She could feel sorry for herself in the refuge of isolation as she licked her wounds. But when the physical attack finally arrived, breaking through the dark shadows of fear that had haunted her for so many years, she had survived! And with that survival, had come a new truth.

No matter how far down she might sink, there was one thing she knew also to be true: A stand must be taken against such narrow-minded hatred. The attack had shown her that it could not be ignored and there was no running from it.

You have to take a stand! And if some self-righteous religious zealot was going to come after her, use her as his symbol to attack, then she would return the favor. She would not allow some insidious hateful scheme created by the narrow-mindedness of bigotry to defeat her or

destroy her and what she had created. She had not come so far to be defeated by such self-righteous piety. For at the depths of the very fiber of her being, she knew with unshakable conviction this truth: Bigotry, the inability to tolerate the differences in others, was one of the great flaws of existence. And she owed it not only to herself, but to so many others who suffered the kind of anguish she had suffered, to fight back.

Suddenly, a renewed power fused through her. Yes, lessons needed to be learned. And she would teach those lessons accompanied by an exacting helping of revenge. This new holier-than-thou nemesis had dropped the gauntlet. So be it! Then let him see what it was like to cross swords with Dragula.

Let the games begin.

She also now saw how wrong she had been to keep secrets from her sister who had been there for her during the attack,...not shying away from the danger, but fighting back. Well, thank you, Rachael. Lesson learned! Secrets were for the weak and afraid. No more secrets! She was determined to make it up to Rachael by telling her everything, come what may.

And there was one more person she needed to see. That policeman who had come to their aid just in the nick of time during "the incident," before something truly horrific could happen. Oh, yes, she wanted to thank him, that went without saying, but .... Well, she had to admit that self-consumed pain-in-the-ass Harry had been right about one thing. Even if José Canusé wanted to do a little "G" Spot entertaining, it probably would not be a politically wise move. And there was always the future, when the time might be more apropos for a Canusé performance. But that policeman.... Now there was something about the way he moved as she watched him run hurriedly away from them.

John Arthur Long

She couldn't quite put her finger on it, but she had an inkling about him.
And she was seldom wrong about such things.

ELEVEN

CURTAIN UP

Police Officer Dick Lacy of the city's mounted patrol division stood at the corner of 8th Avenue and 42nd Street. What was normally a heavy traffic area was much quieter in the wee hours of the morning. In fact, at the moment, it was unusually quiet, quieter than Dick Lacy could ever remember it. Adding to the eerie quiet was another unusual element that was strangely abnormal. A thick fog hung over the area, the combination of heat and humidity in conjunction with the close proximity of the nearby river probably creating such a condition. Still, it was unusual for this section of the city to be blanketed with this type of thick fog, and Dick Lacy made sure he kept alert. Fog created conditions that were ripe for crime, and the prevention of crime was Dick Lacy's business. Forthright and foursquare, if the need was there, Dick Lacy was ready. Just give the call and he was on his way.

Beside him, Dick Lacy's horse whinnied, shaking his mane.

"Easy, Big Fella," Dick muttered, stroking the horse's neck gently. As he did so, in front of him, a red-caped figure materialized out of the fog, walking directly up to him, and an edgy Dick Lacy had his gun in his hand before he consciously realized he had even drawn it from its holster.

"Excuse me, officer."

Dick Lacy lowered the gun, inwardly embarrassed for his edginess. There was something powerful and alluring about this lady in red who had come suddenly out of the fog to confront him, but it was nothing that warranted the need for a gun. She was just a lady, after all.

"You talkin' to me?" Dick Lacy asked.

"Well, we're the only ones here," came her answer. "My, what a big gun you have."

Dick Lacy smiled, putting the pistol back its holster. "Oh, sorry about that. Whatever it takes to protect the public, Ma'am. Just got a little startled. How can I help you?"

"I wanted to thank you for the other night."

"Ah, yes," Dick Lacy replied, suddenly remembering as he took in the woman and her appearance. "Sorry I didn't recognize you at first coming out of the fog the way you did. Sorry to say, I could not locate those who attacked you, though I did try. Are you all right?"

"I'll survive, thanks to you." The woman said. "What's you name?"

"The name's Patrolman Richard Lacy, Ma'am. My friends call me Dick."

Dragula smiled mischievously. "That's really your name? Dick Lacy?"

The policeman smiled shyly. "I know. I've taken my share of ribbing about it. But that's the handle my parents gave me so I guess I've learned to live with it. Glad I was able to help you in your time of need. I always try to be ready."

"Well, my name's Dragula, so, believe me, I understand how people can make fun of a name," the woman said, extending her arm and shaking hands with the officer as she continued to thank him. "And, yes, I was lucky because of you. Just badly shaken up. As I said, you showed up in the nick of time and I really appreciate it."

"They haven't bothered you again, have they?" Lacy questioned.

"No, it was just that one time. Thanks to you I'm sure they are long gone."

Patrolman Lacy smiled. "No trouble at all. That's my job. A cry for help, and I'm on my way, as they say."

"Well, that's good to know," Dragula said, looking around. "But if it's a distant cry for help, how do you get there? I don't see a squad car."

"Don't need one. Got a Hair Trigger," Dick Lacy said proudly.

"Oh, I'm sorry to hear that, " Dragula replied with amusement.

"No need to be." The patrolman crossed to where his horse was tied, patting the animal's head affectionately. "Hair Trigger here's my horse."

"Oh, of course, I should have realized," Dragula replied, taking her own turn at stroking the animal's neck. "He's beautiful."

"We're part of the city's mounted patrol." Dick Lacy continued, patting the horse beside him with pride, his expression taking on a dreamy quality. "Believe me, I love my Hair Trigger. It has helped me in more ways than you can possibly imagine."

"How so...Dick?" Dragula asked, unable to keep a hint of amusement out of her voice.

Dick Lacy turned and pointed off down 42nd Street. "You see those blurry theater marquees all lit up down there? Their shine is dimmed somewhat by the fog, but they're there, all the same. THE GREAT WHITE WAY! That's my dream. Don't get me wrong, I am proud to be part of the city's finest, but show business is my secret calling. My inner desire, you might say. Just once, to be in a musical would be a thrill like no other. Just once to be a part of those tapping feet on 42nd Street. Oh, how I long to hear someone say, 'Let's put on a show!' To be there when the stage manager says, 'Curtain Up!' And step out on the stage...a star! Yup, 'Curtain Up!' That's my dream."

Dragula smiled, wagging a finger as she nodded in response. "I knew it. I knew there was some element of show biz about you. Well, pardon my stupidity, but exactly how does having a Hair Trigger help you?"

"My Hair Trigger taught me how to tap," Dick Lacy answered.

'Really! How so?"

"Well, see, I'd be riding along and I'd be feeling Hair Trigger's strong muscular, moving, sweaty flanks between my tightly clenched thighs, and then, tap...tap...tap! I'd hear Hair Trigger's hooves tapping out the rhythm of the streets. And I'd think...that's it, I can hear those dancing feet! That's how I'll learn to tap. And every time I got down off that horse, I'd give it a try. Tap, tap...tap,tap,tap. Tap, tap...tap, tap, tap."

Dick Lacy pulled the horse's reins over its head, and led it in a circle around them.

"Come on, Hair Trigger," he commanded. "Move those hooves! Get your old Dick up and movin'."

Hair Trigger whinnied in response, and a soft clip-clop of the horse's hooves against the pavement of the street could be heard as the horse trotted in a circle around them. And as the horse moved, Dick Lacy handed the reins to the lady beside him and slowly began a tap routine that concluded with a "Shuffle Off To Buffalo" finale as Hair Trigger whinnied again and Dragula laughed gaily.

"That's really very good," she said, handing the reins back to a blushing Dick Lacy and applauding enthusiastically. "Who would have thought a Hair Trigger could prove so useful?"

Embarrassed, Dick Lacy suddenly became cautious. "Don't you go making fun of me, now. This is my dream."

"Easy...Dick," the woman said, petting the horse's nose. "I think those dancing feet are wonderful. And I think you deserve your

79

chance. But show business is more than just dancing. You've got to be what we refer to in the business as a 'triple threat.' Now, I've got a feel for such things, and I think I know a Dick that can act when I see one, and you're it. But you've got to be able to sing too. Can you sing?"

"Diiiiiiiiiiiiiiiick!" Dick Lacy sang confidently in a soaring tenor voice. "How's that, Ma'am?"

The lady in red smiled. "Well I'm sold. You're a triple threat, no question about it. And it just so happens I have some show business connections, and have been searching for some new talent. Maybe I can help you realize your dream. Would you like to give show biz a try…Dick?"

"Really? I knew there was something special about this night. Imagine, I could finally hear the words, 'Curtain Up!' You wouldn't be fooling me now, would you?"

"Never. You helped me, didn't you? In fact, you saved me! It's the least I can do. You and your Hair Trigger can count on me. It's just a matter of following my lead, and before you know it, you'll hear those magic words, 'Curtain Up!' Of course, you may have to make some changes in your outfit. Would you be willing to do that for a chance to break into show biz?"

Dick Lacy nodded with enthusiasm. "For a chance at show biz? Sure! I've been waiting my whole life for this. It's fate, us meeting the way we did. There's no denying it. How could I refuse? What kind of changes would be required, besides changing out of my uniform, I mean?"

Dragula waved a casual hand. "Oh, just a few minor changes in your appearance."

TWELVE

SNAGULA: ROUND TWO

The Right Reverend Bobby Swagger rubbed his hands together in anticipation. If what he had planned went as well as their first attempt, in a very short time, Dragula and all the sinful corruption she was responsible for spreading would be no more. The trio of Reverend Swagger, Cousin Juicy, and the surprisingly gifted impersonator, Miss Twingle as red-outfitted Dragula, stood huddled together around the corner from The "G" Spot. Swagger motioned for the other two to come closer as he spoke.

"All right, this is it. Time for phase two. Ready, Cousin Juicy?"

"Absolutely. You can count on Cousin Juicy." And as if to prove his point, Cousin Juicy turned to show Swagger the bold printing on the back of the shirt he wore.

"I CAN FIX YOUR CRACK," Swagger read, with a frown of non-comprehension.

"Cousin Juicy Mirror and Glass," the wiry little man clarified, turning front and pointing to the pocket label on his shirt. "Lucky for us, I used to be in the business, and still have some apparel. It will give Miss Twingle and me the perfect cover. No one will be knowing."

"Ah, yes. Clever slogan. And you, Miss Twingle?

Miss Twingle smiled into Swagger's eyes, speaking in her own voice. "It's Tammy, remember?"

"Of course...Tammy. Do you have the Juicy formula?"

Miss Twingle produced a wrapped lollipop and held it upright by the stick in front of her proudly. "Actually, I had Miss Tailgate change it to a lollipop because I thought Dragula would love to...well, you know, and it has a double dose of the special 'mixture,' so one lick and Dragula should go through some very positive changes."

Tammy brought the lollipop in front of her, and Swagger leaned in to read what was printed in large block letters on the wrapper of the lollipop Tammy held waist high.

"Clever thinking, Tammy. Uhh, you've written something on the front of the lollipop wrapper. What does it say?"

"EAT ME, Bobby," Tammy said, her smile widening enthusiastically. "I think it's a good idea, don't you?" Tammy handed Swagger the lollipop to inspect. "I mean, could you resist something that said, 'EAT ME!'?"

Swagger bit his lip as he looked from the lollipop to Miss Twingle. "You're right. Who could resist?"

"You know," Tammy explained. "Like in Alice in Wonderland."

"Ahhhh, of course. Alice in Wonderland," Swagger nodded, finally comprehending his assistant's motivation. "Very good. Quite clever, Ms. Twingle. EAT ME. Of course."

"And I'll do my best, Rev…I mean, Bobby. But this is going to be even harder than acting. Cousin Juicy said this time I may have to do PANT-O-MIME."

Tammy illustrated her meaning with a quick demonstration of the "trapped in the box" pantomime routine that both Cousin Juicy and Swagger watched, exchanging a surprised look of approval as Tammy finished.

"What a reservoir of talent," Swagger said, he and Cousin Juicy providing a quick round of applause. "Do you know, Tammy, I actually thought you were trapped in a closing box for a moment."

Miss Twingle blushed self-consciously as Swagger hugged her encouragingly. "You'll be fine, Miss…I mean Tammy. A bit of mime probably won't even be necessary, but we have to be prepared for all contingencies, and using the mirror repair excuse provides the perfect reason to get you and Cousin Juicy into the club to plant the lollipop in Dragula's dressing room. All right, both of you. Off you go. It's game time!"

After receiving reassuring pats on their backs, Cousin Juicy and Tammy turned to leave, only to be called back almost immediately by Swagger.

"Wait." The Reverend produced a rose as they came back to him. "The flower the doorman mentioned. We can't afford a mistake this time."

Swagger pinned the rose above Tammy's left breast, his hand lingering ever so slightly against the swell of flesh beneath the rose, and then, after the Reverend's approving nod, they turned to leave.

"Wait," Swagger called after them. He held up the lollipop. "You forgot the loaded lollipop."

"Of course. Ohhh, of course. Sorry. I'm just so nervous." Embarrassed, Tammy took the lollipop and she and Cousin Juicy turned again to leave."

"Wait!" Cousin Juicy let out of sigh of exasperation as they turned back to the Reverend yet again. "I wasn't being critical. Just running through our check list. You're going to do fine. Now how about a good luck kiss…Tammy? To help the nerves?"

"Of course…Bobby," Tammy answered, going into Swagger's open arms, for which she received only an affectionate cheek kiss. However, before she could respond with a more meaningful kiss, Swagger had turned her back to her original directions.

"All right, it's time. Best of luck, you two. I'll be right here, Tammy, awaiting the news of your success."

Tammy gave a cute little wave, and then, her expression and physical being shifting to become an impersonation of Dragula, she turned to leave. No fool, however, Cousin Juicy took only two short steps before spinning back around again expectantly.

"All right, let's stop the lollygagging, Cousin Juicy," Swagger instructed, waving them onward. "I know you're nervous, but just follow Tammy's lead and you'll be fine."

Cousin Juicy gave the Reverend a look and then hurried after Tammy who, with a perfect swing-of-the-hips Dragula walk, was already disappearing around the corner.

Seeing Infield sitting on a stool in front of the entrance to The "G" Spot, Cousin Juicy's gait slowed noticeably. However, beside him, Tammy's Dragula stride never missed a step, and she sauntered right up to The "G" Spot bouncer, who smiled and stood as the red-caped figure approached.

Tammy-as-Dragula not only turned on the charm, but also turned Cousin Juicy around and spoke in a perfect imitation of Dragula's voice as she showed Infield the letters printed on the back of the man's shirt.

"He can fix my crack!" Tammy said confidently.

Infield frowned suspiciously. "Huh?"

"He's here to repair a mirror in the dressing room. I'll show him the way."

"Ohhh," Infield said. He eyed Cousin Juicy suspiciously, squeezing the baseball he held in his hand. "Still, I don't know if I should…."

Tammy leaned in to the bouncer. "Did you see the rose I have on today? Isn't it lovely?"

Infield smiled at the flower, relaxing noticeably. "Oh, yeah. A flower. That's a pretty one. Okay, go right in."

The bouncer opened the club's front door, and just like that, the Snagula conspirators entered The "G" Spot.

THIRTEEN

ME, MYSELF, AND I

A quick knock told Cousin Juicy the dressing room was empty. Still, he opened the door just slightly as he called out to be certain there was no one in the room before he entered.

"Hello, Cousin Juicy's Glass and Mirror Service. I can fix your crack? Is anyone in there, please? Hello?"

Reassured by no response, Cousin Juicy slowly stepped into the dressing room. He furtively looked around, and then motioned behind him. Tammy tiptoed into the room, glancing around and taking in the surroundings. She crossed and looked affectionately at the vase of orchids on the dressing table as Cousin Juicy pulled a tall folding floral-patterned changing screen to beside the dressing table, and motioned for Tammy to hide behind it.

"Hurry," Cousin Juicy said in an anxious whisper. "Someone may come at any moment. We must move quickly. I will remove the mirror. You leave the loaded lolly."

"No, I thought the mirror excuse was just to get us in here. You can't take the mirror," Tammy objected, with a whisper of intensity that matched Cousin Juicy's. "Dragula will know something is wrong the minute she comes in and sees the mirror gone. She'll never lick the lolly."

Cousin Juicy flicked the switch that lit the bright round bulbs around the mirror. "Oh, no, I must take the mirror. Last time I came in the back and no one saw me. This time, however, you brought me in the front. Now, the doorman knows we're here. Carrying the mirror is the only way I will get out of here undetected."

He pointed to the large rectangular mirror framed within the surrounding glowing round bulbs as he worked at unfastening the reflecting glass from its hinges.

"Look, the intense light blocks out all except the image directly in front of the mirror. Now if Dragula sits, you slide from behind to the open space and imitate the actions opposite you exactly as in pantomime. You can do it! After seeing your 'trapped in a box' routine, I know you can. It's the only way. With the intense lighting, it will work perfectly. After Dragula takes the lolly, she will undoubtedly be experiencing a certain amount of disorientation as the formula takes hold. When that happens, you simply slip out of the dressing room and leave the club. No one will stop you because they will think you are she. No one will be knowing. It will work perfectly. You can depend on Cousin Juicy."

"But what if Dragula switches off the light? She'll know immediately something's up when she sees a large rectangular hole where her mirror should be."

"She won't do that. Performers love to look at themselves. Believe me. The lights will stay on until the lolly is licked. Then it does not matter."

"Okay," Tammy said, her expression filled with doubt. "If you're sure it will work."

"Absolutely. The intensity of the lighted bulbs is the key. Remember there is only a reflection when someone sits directly in front of it. So, you only have to worry if Dragula actually sits down. If she licks the lolly without ever sitting, you simply sneak out. If she sits before licking, however, you will have to employ your expert pantomime skills. Just be sure you mime the actions exactly, and it will not fail."

Nodding, Tammy hurried towards the mirror Cousin Juicy was unfastening, and placed the lollipop on the dressing table top in front of Dragula's chair. Then she grabbed another chair from the corner of the room and carried it in back of the table to behind the mirror, sitting down as Cousin Juicy removed the mirror from its frame.

"How do I look?" Tammy said in her Dragula voice as her image filled the open rectangular space inside the glowing bulbs where the mirror had been.

Cousin Juicy nodded, wide-eyed, as he gazed at her image surrounded by the light bulbs. "Amazing. It's better than I imagined. This might actually work."

Tammy tilted her Dragula-wigged head within the glowing light and frowned. "Hey. I thought you said this could not fail."

"Of course. That is right. No one will be knowing." Clearly anxious to leave, Cousin Juicy adjusted his grip on the large rectangular mirror in his hands. "Okay. Get behind the changing screen. I've got the mirror. I'm going."

Tammy ran out from behind the screen, answering in a loud slow exaggerated whisper. "Okay. I'll...make...sure...Dragula...licks...the...lol...ly. And as soon as I'm sure of success, I'll sneak out of here, and our job is done."

Tammy gave the wiry little man a conspiratorial wink and, with a hurried return wink, Cousin Juicy moved out the door, calling to anyone he might encounter as he exited. "Excuse please. Cousin Juicy Mirror and Glass...I can fix your crack,...Coming through. Excuse please."

Left alone, Tammy closed the door to the dressing room, and tiptoed behind the screen, where she stood very still...waiting.

For several long minutes nothing happened. However, resisting the urge to peek out from behind the screen became more and more difficult for the vivacious Dragula impersonator as the minutes dragged by. Finally, unable to stand the wait any longer, Tammy slowly inched her way to the edge of the changing screen and was right in the middle of poking her head around the edge of the screen to take a look into the room when suddenly the door swung open, and she jerked her head and body back from view before she could see that Peter, not in his Dragula costume, but rather in dressing gown and hairnet, had entered the room.

A panicked Tammy Twingle knew only one thing. The sound of the approaching footsteps moving across the room indicated the figure was headed for the chair at the dressing table. She braced herself, ready for the moment she had dreaded. Phase two of Snagula was not going to take place the easy way, after all. She was going to be called upon right from the start to make it work. It was mime time.

She counted the steps and listened. Closer, so very much closer, came the footfalls. Then the steps stopped. The figure was at the chair. Tammy measured the seconds, visualizing the figure's movement. She could not get it wrong. There would be no second chance. The success of Snagula rested solely on her shoulders, and she could not...correction, she would not let Reverend...correction...Bobby... down.

One, two, three, four. Now! With fingers crossed, Tammy ducked, slid sideways into the chair, and faced front just as the person who had entered the room sat down in the chair opposite her.

Then came the moment of overwhelming panic. The person sitting in front of the blazing lights before her was not Dragula!

Just as the person across from her turned to look in the "mirror,"

Tammy saw that it was not Dragula in wig and dress opposite her,

89

but a young man wearing a hairnet and dressing gown. Realizing her mistake in the split second that it took the figure to turn toward the mirror, she leaped back behind the screen. Simultaneously, a noise of "G" Spot performers laughing and talking as they moved down the hallway outside the room caused the person sitting in front of her to look away from the mirror and stand, crossing back to the doorway to close the door.

Tammy stood hovering behind the changing screen, fingers crossed and shoulders scrunched, biting her lower lip, hoping that the person had not seen her.

At the closed doorway, Peter stopped. He paused momentarily, turned his head and frowned, looking back toward the dressing table. Slowly, a smile materialized on his face replacing the frown, and Peter crossed back to the dressing table, stopping in front of it, looking not at the lighted mirror area in front of him, but rather down at a lone lollipop that lay on the polished formica top before him.

"Hmmm, how strange," Peter said aloud, picking up the lollipop. "A lollipop. What's this writing on the wrapper? EAT ME! A little trip into Wonderland, eh. Sounds intriguing."

Behind the changing screen, Tammy Twingle's heart pounded with excitement. He had the lolly. But it was all wrong. It wasn't Dragula. She listened to the sound of paper being unwrapped. Oh, god. He was unwrapping the loaded lolly. What should she do? And then the sucking sounds and dreaded words came that told her that there was nothing she could do. It was too late. The double dose of juicy formula was being licked and sucked.

John Arthur Long

"Ummm," Peter's voice said. "What an interesting taste. I can't quite place it. But it is pleasant. I'll just have a few licks now, and save the rest for later. It's always good to save a few licks for later on."

Hearing movement, Tammy decided to chance it, and sneak a peek. Veerrryyy carefully, she edged her way to the end of the changing screen and dared a look. The young man had his back to her, and was moving across the dressing room to the closet. He opened the closet, and took off his dressing gown.

What she saw caused a flood of relief to pass through Tammy Twingle, for under the dressing gown, the figure was wearing none other than the Dragula dress. It was Dragula, after all! And Dragula had licked the lolly. They were saved. All she had to do now was watch for the results and leave, hurrying back to Bobby with a "mission accomplished" message, and in turn receive what would probably prove to be the best, most passionate-filled hug so far.

From the closet shelf, Tammy watched the figure select a Dragula wig. So far, there had been no reaction from the lolly lick, and Tammy knew she probably should wait to see actual proof of the results, but the Dragula impersonator also knew that if she were going to make a break for it, now was the time, while the other person's back was to her.

Deciding that, considering the circumstances, fate had already been more than kind to her and that remaining would be pushing her luck beyond all reasonable limits, Tammy made her move. As quietly as possible, she started to edge her way around the screen so that she could bolt for the door before the figure turned.

However, just as she started to move, without warning, Dragula suddenly spun around, hurrying toward the dressing table as she pulled the wig over her hairnet and sat down. Knowing there was no

91

choice, simultaneously, Tammy ducked, slid sideways, and sat in the chair on the opposite side, pulling at her wig and adjusting it in perfect synchronized imitation of the figure across from her as Dragula settled into her chair and gazed into the "mirror" before her.

Slowly the figure across from her, while smiling and keeping their gazes locked, reached to the vase of orchids on the dressing table and selected a flower. Still caught in the habit of mimicry that she had fallen into, Tammy reached for the vase on her side with a duplicate motion, though she knew the gesture was futile. There was no vase of orchids on her side, and when her hand moved back across the brilliant light of the bulbs to the open space before her, unlike the slender fingers that held an exquisite blood red orchid in the hand opposite her, Tammy's hand was empty. The impersonator dropped her eyes to the rose Bobby had fastened to her dress, and looked back up to meet the knowing eyes of Dragula.

"Oh, I tried so hard. But this game of Snagula is doomed."

"Come out here, my dear," Dragula said, waving her around the dressing table.

Tammy rose and crossed around to stand beside Dragula. What else could she do?

"Don't feel bad," Dragula said, scooting back her chair and standing beside Tammy. "You actually do me very well. You really were very good. And I loved your note on the lollipop."

As Dragula uttered the word "lollipop," her body suddenly froze. Hope blossomed anew in Tammy Twingle as she watched a convulsion pass through the figure beside her. Dragula spun around once as Tammy gasped, and then just as suddenly, the star performer of The "G" Spot stopped and smiled, completely in control.

"Just kidding, Tammy," Dragula said with a throaty laugh. "But nice try. Still, you didn't really expect it to work, did you? After all, I am Dragula, you know. And my doorman was nice enough to tell me all about your little deception game which I now understand completely." She turned to the door and opened it. "Oh, boys. Could you come in here for a minute?"

Infield, the bouncer, and Renarde, The "G" Spot emcee, came smiling into the room. They moved to either side of Tammy-as-Dragula, took off her rose and switched it with Dragula's orchid.

"Inny and Renarde are going to keep you company for a while, Tammy, my dear, while I pay a little visit to the Reverend, who, I believe, is anxiously awaiting your return. Won't he be surprised when he finds out I'm you." She smiled, fastening the rose to her bodice. "I think I'm beginning to enjoy this little game of Snagula, as you called it."

Dragula started for the door, then stopped and turned back to the pouting Tammy.

"I've failed. How will I ever face Reverend Swagger again?" Tammy whined, bursting into tears.

"Oh, now don't be upset, Tammy. You did your best. But consider who you're up against. Just sit down and relax. I won't be long." Dragula picked up the lollipop from the table and offered it to Tammy. "Oh, and if you get hungry, here's a lollipop you can suck on while you're waiting for me to get back. Personally, I never suck...." Dragula paused with a smile for just the right number of beats. "unless I know exactly what it is I'm sucking on. And you tell the boys if you need anything, because they're going to keep a very close eye on you until I return."

With a smile to Infield and Renarde, the red-caped drag queen swept dramatically out the dressing room door. And poor Tammy Twingle, dejected but still looking like the Dragula she had tried so hard to fool, sank under the glare of the mirror bulbs around her in ironic defeat into entertainer's dressing room chair.

FOURTEEN

SOME GIRLS JUST LOVE TO KISS AND TELL

"Whoohoo…Reverend Swagger!"

Bobby Swagger had been pacing anxiously back and forth when he heard the call. He stopped and looked in the direction of the cry. It was night, and a low fog had settled over the area. Still, he could see well enough by the streetlight illumination to spot the red-caped figure as it materialized out of the fog and moved down the sidewalk toward him.

"Ahhh. Tammy, at last," Swagger shouted to her. "I've been all atwitter waiting to hear."

They hurried toward each other. Swagger stepping quickly and then almost running while Dragula did her best to imitate the movements and overall demeanor of the Reverend's assistant. There was no doubt in her mind that she could fool him. She was Dragula, the star performer of The "G" Spot, wasn't she? The day she couldn't fool the likes of a narrow-minded bigot like Bobby Swagger would be the day.

A wide smile on his face, Swagger stopped short when he reached the lady in red, his body not quite touching hers.

"You look awfully happy, Tammy," he said. "Does that mean what I think it means?"

Dragula-as-Tammy nodded her head shyly. "Ummmhmmm.

"DRAGULA LICKED THE LOLLIPOP?"

"Sucked on it like there was no tomorrow," Dragula-as-Tammy confirmed.

"Wonderful! Wonderful! Well, tell me everything. What happened?"

"Why, Reverend Swagger," Dragula-as-Tammy cooed with a flutter of eyelashes. "Don't I get a thank-you first? It wasn't easy, you know…all that pantomime and everything."

Swagger gave the lovely lady beside him a flirting grin. "Of course. And it's Bobby, remember?"

"I mean…Bobby."

Swagger extended his arms. "How about a big thank-you kiss? Would that fill the bill?"

Dragula-as-Tammy stepped into Swagger's open arms. "That will more than fill the bill…Bobby."

"Then pucker up 'cause here comes Bobby to deliver a great big thank-you smackeroonee!"

Dragula-as-Tammy leaned forward innocently, butt out, head forward and lips pursed. However, Swagger, ever-in-charge, grabbed her and gathered her within the fold of his arms. They embraced in a long passionate kiss, Dragula's leg lifting and rubbing against Swagger, whose eyes opened momentarily in delighted surprise and then closed again as he kissed the woman in his arms with even greater passion. Finally, the embrace broke, and Swagger staggered back slightly, his breath short, coming in quick gasps of throbbing emotion.

"That…that was quite a kiss, Tammy. More than I expected. Where did you learn to kiss like that, pray tell?"

Though Dragula-as-Tammy smiled with coquettish shyness, her face was flushed with surprise at the passion that ignited had between them when they kissed. "I guess you just inspired me, Bobby. And, now that you've given me a thank-you, I think I should reciprocate with a kiss for all that you've done to me. What do you think? Shall we have another go at it?"

Swagger blushed with arousal. "Well, if you insist...Tammy."

"Oh, I do...Bobby."

Taking command, Dragula-as-Tammy grabbed Swagger and kissed him passionately, her hands going behind his back, grasping the cheeks of his buttocks and pulling him into her as they embraced. Finally, after many long passion-filled moments, Dragula broke the kiss without warning and backed away, Swagger following, his arms grasping to hold her.

"Oh, Tammy. Your...your tongue was so exciting. I don't think I've ever experienced anything quite like it. Oh, Tammy. I need you. I want you. Perhaps we could go somewhere."

Dropping the Tammy persona, Dragula backed away slightly, breathing hard and yet refusing to give in to the arousal of emotion that had surfaced from kissing the man who is her opponent,...her enemy. Steeling her resolve, Dragula gave the approaching Swagger a strong shove that, catching him unawares, sent him staggering backwards.

"Over my dead body, Bobby!"

Swagger regained his footing and shook his head in confusion. "What? No, Tammy, please, there's no need for the Dragula impression anymore." He moved closer as he spoke. "Thanks to you, it's all over. We've won!"

"On the contrary, you couldn't be more wrong, Swagger. And I'm sure your dear sweet Tammy will tell you all about it when she gets here."

Swagger staggered back away from the red-caped figure before him, suddenly afraid. "What? What are you saying?"

But there was no verbal response. The lady-in-red simply smiled.

"Oh, no…OH, NO!" Swagger cried in realization, his fist going to his gaping mouth. "DRAGULA! Good Lord, I've been kissing Dragula!"

Dragula smiled. "The one and only, Big Boy. And I know a girl really shouldn't kiss and tell, but I can't wait!"

"No, it can't be." Swagger shook his head, unable to believe what he was hearing. "Tammy, you stop it now. This isn't funny."

"You mean it wasn't funny, you scheming pontificator. How do you like playing Snagula now, hmmm? Because you're dead wrong, Reverend. Now it is funny. Now it is very funny indeed!"

"No, it can't be," Swagger moaned in horror. "It can't be!"

"Oh, I'm afraid it can be, Reverend. And is!"

"Oh, good lord, no!" Swagger gasped.

Dragula laughed heartily as she walked away from him. "By the way, just so you know for the next time, even though there isn't going to be a next time, I always wear an orchid, not a rose."

Then, suddenly, Dragula stopped. With a sigh, she turned and crossed back to the still dumbfounded Reverend Swagger.

"If I ask you something, will you be totally honest with me?"

"Of course," Swagger answered, regaining a semblance of composure. "I am a man of God, after all. If we can't trust a minister, who can we trust?"

Dragula rolled her eyes. "All right…and you can thank my sister for this because she thinks I should be more open with others, so I promised myself I'd try. I'll admit it's a little ironic that I'm starting with you, but this seems to be as good as time as any…especially considering what just happened between us."

"Well, that was…a misunderstanding. I thought…."

"I know what you thought, Reverend," Dragula said. "I'm talking about what actually happened."

Swagger frowned, hesitating. "I...I don't get you."

"Oh, I think you do. Maybe this whole thing is a...misunderstanding. I've never done anything to you, have I? I mean, this Snagula business. Is it really worth all this effort? Why do you hate me so much?"

Swagger seemed caught off guard by Dragula's question. "Well, I...I don't hate you."

"Nor I you. I'll admit I find your beliefs are a tad distorted, but otherwise, you're not so bad, once one gets past all the religious prattle. In fact, you have a wonderful, commanding presence and appear to be in very good physical shape. Do you work out?"

Flattered, Swagger straightened, his chest swelling. "Well, I try not to let myself go."

Dragula moved closer to Swagger, who did not move away.

"Well, I think that's exactly what you should do, if you don't mind my saying so."

Swagger frowned, shifting with uncertainty. "Meaning...?"

"Let yourself go!" Dragula said, smiling. "Because there's something very exciting inside there, just waiting to break free. Took me by surprise, believe me! But I felt it. And I know you felt it too. You just said as much."

"I...I thought you were...Miss Twingle."

Dragula touched his arm. "Well, I'm not. So, then you didn't feel anything just now when we...?"

Swagger took a breath. "Miss Dragula, I...I am willing to admit that in the moment, I...."

"Peter," Dragula interrupted, the vocal tone dropping in pitch.

"I'm sorry?"

"My name is Peter. For the time being anyway, you can call me Peter, Bobby, if we're going to continue to spend time together and get to the bottom of all this. And I'm thinking we should. You know, to sort of clear the air and...whatever...."

"Well, I'm not saying that's not an option at this point, but if it were, I'm afraid I'd have to point out to you the error of your ways,..Peter...Your name is Peter?"

Dragula smiled. "For the time being. And I think first names are best, Bobby...while we work on letting ourselves go." Before Swagger could object, Dragula leaned in and gave the Reverend a quick cheek kiss. Then turned, took a couple of steps away, and turned back, the voice once again feminine and alluring. "Let's both think about it, all right? Oh, and thanks for the smooch compliment. Of course, I hear that from all the boys. Bye for now!"

Laughing, Dragula turned once again and her figure swaying sensuously, waved over her shoulder, disappearing around the corner as Swagger stared after her. Then, with a shudder, he gasped and sank to his knees.

"OH, MY GOD! THIS TIME IT WASN'T A MISTAKE! IT REALLY HAPPENED! I KISSED DRAGULA!" the Right Reverend Bobby Swagger cried, lifting his clenched hands to the heavens in despair. "But how could it have felt so wonderful? Good lord, what is happening to me? I've got to get ahold of myself. This...this is all wrong." Swagger struggled to stand, coming unsteadily to his feet. "Lord, give me strength. How could I have liked it so much? It has to be because I though it was Miss Twingle and I was yielding to temptation. Yes, that must be it! That's why Dragula suddenly seemed so,...so appealing. Yield not to temptation for yielding's a sin, the scriptures tell us. Could it be that God is punishing me with false feelings because I gave into the sin of lust! And yet, she was so nice and understanding and…appealing. But, wait,…she said her name is Peter. Not Dragula, but Peter! But, only Peter for the time being? What does that mean? That she is a he? Or he a she? How could I have been so wrong? How could I have been?"

Swagger suddenly stood stock still as a new realization came to him.

"WAIT! Maybe…MAYBE SHE'S ENTRAPPING ME! YES! Of course, THAT HAS TO BE IT," Swagger cried, sinking once more to his knees. "Oh, Lord, forgive me for my sinful transgression! But, thank you for showing me the error of my ways."

FIFTEEN

WALKING THE STRAIGHT AND NARROW

As Reverend Swagger attempted to gain control of his emotions and struggled to stand once more, his hands clasped in prayer, the exuberant Cousin Juicy came rushing across the street. However, the wiry little man momentarily lost his usual glad-handed nature when he watched the Reverend getting to his feet, and he hurried to Swagger's assistance.

"Reverend, what is it?" Cousin Juicy questioned, lending a helping hand. "You do not look well. Has Miss Twingle returned yet?"

Swagger struggled for composure as he wiped at his lips over and over and spat at the pavement in unconcealed disgust. "No, not yet. I...I'm still waiting. It's been a long while, too long, in fact. I'm not hopeful, I'm afraid."

Swagger brushed irritably at his rumpled clothing as he shook his head. Before Cousin Juicy could make a reply, Tammy Twingle came hurrying down the sidewalk toward them. This lady in red, however, was clearly frightened and kept glancing behind her as she emerged into view out of the fog-filled night. With head bowed, her pace slowed as she approached the men who awaited her.

"I think you are right, Reverend," Cousin Juicy said as he watched Tammy approach. "This does not look good. Ms. Twingle, what happened?"

Tammy did not answer Cousin Juicy as she came to a halt in front of the two men. Instead, she lifted her head and met Swagger's gaze. "You know?"

"Yes," Swagger sighed. "I know. Dragula was here."

Tammy's eyes filled. "I'm...I'm sorry, Bobby."

Reverend Swagger squared his shoulders, took a deep breath and put his arm around the distressed assistant. However, it was a hug of comfort only, devoid of passion.

"It's all right, Miss Twingle," the Reverend said, his tone coated with parental understanding. "You gave it your best. I couldn't ask for more than that from anyone. We just underestimated our adversary, that's all."

"So then the loaded lolly did not work?" Cousin Juicy asked.

It was a sniffling Tammy who answered with a shake of her head. "Dragula refused. Can you imagine? He refused to suck or even lick it. Far more clever than we imagined, I'm afraid."

Never one to dwell on failures as he looked for new opportunities, Cousin Juicy shrugged. "Well, win some, lose some. You gave it a good try, Reverend."

Swagger's chin lifted in the air, the glare of his stare making it clear that he was not one to accept defeat so easily.

"WHAT? DO YOU THINK I'M GOING TO STOP NOW? DO YOU THINK NOW THAT I HAVE BEHELD THIS FIEND'S CRAFTINESS, I WILL SIMPLY WALK AWAY?" As he spoke, Bobby Swagger's voice filled with a revivalist's emotion. "DO YOU THINK NOW THAT I HAVE SEEN THE "G" SPOT AND WHAT GOES ON THERE, I CAN EVER GO BACK TO INTERCOURSE? NEVER! We just underestimated our opponent. But it won't happen again. Next time we'll know better. We'll just have to find a different approach, that's all."

A man who had mastered the ability to shift with the changing direction of the wind, Cousin Juicy nodded. "Okay. You could always go back to Tailgate. I'm sure she's got something else that might help."

His eyes ablaze with a renewed resolve, Swagger did a slow turn to Cousin Juicy. "Of course. That's it. Good thinking, Cousin Juicy. What was it she said about coming back when one needed other things? That must mean she has other weapons we can use. Other things that are even more effective than the juicy formula the bitches concocted."

Cousin Juicy gave the Reverend a crafty smile. "Sure she does, but more expensive. I know Tailgate. This time you'll pay big, believe me."

"Damn the price!" Swagger boomed, pacing with new energy and excitement. "No amount is too much to stop this monster. I'll use the congregation's tithing to the church if I have to. It's completely justified in a battle of this magnitude. Yes, that's it. We'll go back to Tailgate, and get a weapon that will stop this disciple of the devil once and for all! But it's got to be good, because this time the fiend will be ready for us. We'll have to get the best weapon Tailgate's got. Are ya with me, Miss Twingle?"

Tammy pulled the back of her hand across her face, wiping at her tears, and squared her shoulders, her ample chest held high. Clearly a man of fresh resolve, Swagger's gaze never strayed, except for a quick surreptitious glance downward, from his assistant's face.

"Yes...Reverend," Tammy said. "But to tell you the truth, I thought Dragula was surprisingly pleasant. She didn't even seem that angry about our game of Snagula. I mean, she just doesn't seem all that bad to me."

"Do not let her fool you, Miss Twingle. I'll admit she can be persuasive. Why, I actually found myself momentarily attracted to her, slipping toward her sensual attractiveness, if you can believe it. But, with the Lord's help, I have seen the error of my ways. And if I can resist her seductive ways, Miss Twinge, so can you. Now, I ask you again. Are you with me?"

"If you can be confident after what's happened, so can I," Tammy replied with determination.

Swagger nodded. "That's my girl. And what about you, Cousin Juicy? Are you with us?"

"Oh, yes, if there is going to be money as you say, you can count on Cousin Juicy," the man grinned, nodding his head in agreement.

"Then let us speak our resolve aloud," Swagger urged with evangelistic zeal. "We may have hit a little bump in the road, but it has only strengthened my determination. For I say to you here tonight, we will walk the straight and narrow, and we will not fail. Oh, yes, the world offers temptations, and I know them all too well. But I choose to go to heaven, while everyone else can go to hell."

"Why, that sounds like gospel preaching, Reverend," Tammy said, a newfound happiness in her demeanor. "Whether it's gospel preaching or gospel singing, I just love gospel!"

"No, Miss Twingle," Swagger corrected. "This is not gospel. This is serious conviction. I do not condone gospel. Gospel is too much fun. And fun leads to temptation, lascivious living, and the devil's play. And we cannot, I say, we cannot have fun. We cannot enjoy ourselves and fall prey to those temptations. Yes, Miss Twingle, I will admit that I fell prey to temptation when we embraced. But I have seen the evil of my temptation. When Dragula came to me earlier, I allowed the temptation of the moment to take me, and I was led to the doorway, Miss Twingle. I stood on the very doorstep to hell. But I cannot...no, strike that...I will not follow that path! So when you hear my words, and when you repeat my words, it may feel and sound like gospel, but do not yield to the temptation of enjoyment. When we speak, no, not speak,..when we sing our faith and conviction to heaven, as with all things, we must walk the straight and narrow. It can be no other way."

Having worked himself into a fervor of religious passion, Reverend Swagger waved his arms to a Salvation Army volunteer standing at a storefront, playing a portable keyboard.

"Join us, brother," Swagger shouted, beckoning the man to them. "Bring your instrument and join us as we sing our conviction to the Lord." And with that, the words pouring from him, Reverend Swagger raised his voice and sang.

♫ "For the world offers temptations,
And I know them all too well.

But I choose to go to heaven
While everyone else can go to hell.

Because I'm walking the straight and narrow.
From this path I will not stray.

I feel it right down to my marrow,
And there's nothin' more to say.

Others may fall to sin and sorrow.
They may try the Devil's play.

But I'm walking the straight and narrow,
And there is no other way.

You may tempt me with hard liquor,
and the pleasures of the flesh.

But I'm walking free of sinnin',
where the path is always fresh.

So take all your lascivious conduct,
and please walk the other way.

Because my soles are shod with moral souls,
and there is no other way."

Suddenly Swagger froze in position, his singing stopped and he lifted his hands toward heaven.

"WAIT! IT HAS COME TO ME! A DIVINE INSPIRATION AS I SANG THE WORDS OF THE LORD. I HAVE SEEN THE LIGHT! A MESSAGE FROM GOD, IF YOU WILL! I KNOW WHAT I NEED TO SHOW THE FIEND, DRAGULA, THE ERROR OF HER WAYS!"

"Praise the Lord," Tammy said, her own arms lifting to join Swagger. "What is it?"

"A HERMAPHRODITE!" Swagger shouted.

"A WHAT?" Tammy asked, taken aback.

"A HERMAPHRODITE! Don't you see? If confronted with a hermaphrodite, she cannot help but see how wrong it all is. Oh, praise Jesus! Thank you, Lord, for showing me the way! But a hermaphrodite! Where on Earth would I ever find such a thing?"

Cousin Juicy's expression was deadpan as he spoke to Swagger.

"I think I might be able to help you out with that one, Reverend."

SIXTEEN

MA DADDY

The Three Bitches were very busy cleaning and polishing juice bottles and shelves when Tailgate came rushing up from her office to the front counter of the New Age Health Bar.

"GIRLS, LISTEN," shouted Tailgate, interrupting the workers before they could finish with their cleaning jobs, which irritated them to no end. They would have started bitching about that immediately, but Tailgate, knowing the three only too well, didn't give them the chance.

Before any of the bitches could even attempt to get a word in edgewise, she said, "I just heard from…."

Stopping suddenly and looking around, Tailgate surprised even herself by pausing in what she was saying as she saw all the gleaming bottles.

"Ewwwww. Nice job, girls," Tailgate said, knowing it was a mistake to leave the Bitches an opening, but unable to stop herself from pausing to admire their work. "There's nothing like a good cleaning to lift one's spirits, is there?"

The First Bitch spoke up, pointing with her feather duster for emphasis, and Tailgate instantly regretted her mistake. "I think my dusting did the trick, don't you, Tailgate? These two Bitches were just bitching about what a lousy job I was doing."

"We were not, you bitch," bitched Bitch Two. "It was my waxing that brought out the luster around this place."

Bitch Three made a face at Bitch Two, and squirted a nearby Juice bottle with a shot of lemon-fresh wax spray, rubbing the glass until it gleamed in the light. "You're the bitch! My polishing work is so good that I can see my delicate facial features reflected in the glass of this bottle. Tell these bitches I'm right, Tailgate."

"Pretty cocksure of yourself, aren't you, bitch," retorted the first bitch before Tailgate could say anything.

"GIRLS, STOP IT!" Tailgate shouted. "STOP BITCHING FOR A MINUTE AND LISTEN! This is important! I just got a call from Cousin Juicy."

As Tailgate well knew, the mention of Cousin Juicy's name was all that was needed, and the bitching was replaced immediately by pouty excitement.

"Oh, Cousin Juicy," Bitch One cooed. "We love to squeeze the Juicy!"

Tailgate nodded, hurrying on before any bitching started about who liked Cousin Juicy the most. "I know. And you can squeeze Cousin Juicy all you want, I promise. But first, there's work to be done. Because guess what else? He's baaaccckkk!"

"Who? Reverend Swagger?" guessed the second Bitch.

"That's right. Just like I told you. And guess what else? As luck would have it, he is looking for a,...hermaphrodite!"

The Three Bitches looked at each other in stunned silence for a moment and then shouted. "WAIT! WE'VE GOT A HERMAPHRODITE!"

"I knooowww!" Tailgate said with a roll of her eyes as the bitches began to jump around in uncontrollable excitement. "And we've got to make sure we convince him we've got what he needs so this time he'll really pay. So be ready. When I ask, make sure you sell it like you've never sold anything before. And...."

"We know," the Bitches put in, before Tailgate could finish. "No bitching."

The Bitches giggled like schoolgirls, hurriedly stowing their cleaning implements out of sight in the back area behind the drawn curtain, and then skipped around the shop, tidying up. Suddenly, they froze in anticipation as the entrance bell jingled, and Cousin Juicy entered, followed by Reverend Swagger and Tammy Twingle.

"Hello, Bitches!" Cousin Juicy said good-naturedly. "Are you happy to see me?"

Squealing with delight, the Bitches rushed over to Juicy as Tailgate gave Swagger a strong welcoming handshake.

"Welcome back to our little establishment, Reverend," she said, turning to Tammy to give her hand a squeeze. "And how are you feeling, Tammy? Need a sweet lift from an energy Juicy?"

"Maybe later, Miss Tailgate," Tammy answered. "But right now we need to help Reverend Swagger because the formula didn't do the trick. We need something much more powerful for Dragula, and Cousin Juicy says...."

"Yes," Cousin Juicy added quickly, exchanging a look with Tailgate as he continued. "I thought Reverend Swagger could inquire about...Ma Daddy."

"...MA DADDY!" Tailgate said in shocked surprise.

Swagger frowned. "You seem somewhat...apprehensive. Why? Is there a problem?"

Tailgate shook her head, hesitating, calling the bitches over to them. "I'll have to let the girls explain that one. The Reverend wants to know about Ma Daddy. How would you describe Ma Daddy, ladies?"

All three Bitches stepped toward Swagger, but Bitch One was the first to speak, her tone ominous and dark.

"Who is Ma Daddy? Wait till you see. It's scary as can be!"

"Who is Ma Daddy?" added Bitch Two. "It isn't very nice. But it'll do your bidding, if you pay the price."

"Who is Ma Daddy? continued Bitch Three. "It'll make you quake with fear. People shake and run away whenever it is near. Ma Daddy is big, it's bad, it's mean...."

"Yes," put in Bitch Two. "Ma Daddy's the worst you've ever seen."

"But can I use Ma Daddy? How will it help me in my quest?" a frustrated Swagger questioned.

"Well, you have to pay for Ma Daddy," Tailgate answered, taking over for the Bitches now that money was an issue. "But if you're willing to pay, the answer is yes."

Swagger paused, wanting to be sure. "Well..., Cousin Juicy seemed to indicate...I mean, I need to be sure. How can this Ma Daddy help me? Who is Ma Daddy?"

"Oh, sorry, I thought you knew," Tailgate answered with exaggerated casualness. "Ma Daddy is a hermaphrodite."

Swagger gasped in wonder. "A hermaphrodite. MA DADDY IS THE HERMAPHRODITE!"

"Oh, yes," Cousin Juicy added quickly. "Sorry for the confusion. Ma Daddy is the hermaphrodite. A very strange thing indeed. It has both sexes, you know."

"I know. I KNOW," Swagger answered, his excitement growing with each word. "MISS TWINGLE, DO YOU HEAR? EXACTLY WHAT WE NEED! GOD BE PRAISED! IT'S A MIRACLE! The Lord sent me the revelation and now has delivered the answer to my prayers!

All right! Damn the price!" Swagger continued. "If it's as bad as you say it is, it's just what Dragula needs to be confronted with the realization of the horrific distortion she has become. What's the fee? And when can I see this Ma Daddy?"

"As luck would have it, Reverend," Tailgate said, "we have the pleasure of Ma Daddy being with us this very day. I can take you to Ma Daddy now, if you'd like."

Swagger smiled to Cousin Juicy and Tammy, nodding his agreement. "Perfect! And the fee?"

Tailgate didn't even hesitate with her answer. "Five thousand dollars."

"Ohhh, that's a lot more than the formula,'" Tammy said.

"Yes," Tailgate answered. "And worth every penny, I assure you."

Swagger, however, not one to make a foolhardy snap decision, was taking his time before committing to such a large sum and, as he considered, the Bitches leaned forward and spoke to urge him on.

"Ma Daddy's biiiiig," Bitch One said.

"Ma Daddy's baaaad," Bitch Two added.

"Ma Daddy's meeeean," Bitch Three concluded.

They looked at each other and then back to Swagger, nodding.

"Ma Daddy's the worst you've ever seen!"

"THEN TAKE ME TO MA DADDY, BITCHES!" Swagger announced with unflappable conviction. "If it's all you say it is, it's worth any price! And I have a plan on how we can make this work! But I'll need all of you. Could Cousin Juicy's Mirror and Glass come up with some mirrors if I needed them?"

Cousin Juicy grinned and shrugged as if the question were a foregone conclusion. "You can count on Cousin Juicy, Reverend."

"I'll need you also, Tailgate, and the Bitches too if I'm going to make this work. If I pay this surprisingly high price, can I count on all of you as well as Ma Daddy to execute my plan?"

Tailgate took Swagger's arm. "Right this way, Reverend. To quote your friend and mine, Cousin Juicy, you can count on us. And you won't regret this decision. Hold down the fort, girls, while I introduce the Reverend here to Ma Daddy."

The bitches watched with suppressed delight as Tailgate escorted Swagger, Tammy and Cousin Juicy off to behind the curtained area and through the back hallway that led to the rooms beyond the counter. Once the group had disappeared, the Bitches leaped for joy.

"We've got five thousand dollars! We've got five thousand dollars," the Bitches chanted happily, skipping arm-in-arm.

"Personally, I thought I was the best convincer," said Bitch One.

"My Ma Daddy convincer did the trick and you know it, bitch," disagreed Bitch Two.

"Wrong. My performance was the convincer. You bitches just can't admit it."

"Hey, bitches," realized Bitch Two. "It doesn't matter. We've got five thousand dollars! Ain't that a bitch!"

And nodding together, the Three Bitches, in harmony for one of the few times in their lives, gleefully raised their hands and high-fived each other over and over, punctuating each slap with cackles of pleasure and the phrase, "Ain't that a bitch!"

SEVENTEEN

CURTINNA UPP WITH TWO Ps

"Wonderful, Darlings," Renarde called, taking the ensemble of "G" Spot performers through their rehearsal for the night's show. "Keep it up! Again. Tap, kick, tap, tap, kick. Tap, kick, tap, tap, tap, kick. Wonderful."

Renarde was dressed in a pink rehearsal leotard with matching sweat band and towel, moving from group to group as the members of the troupe worked on their routines to the musical accompaniment of Ivory Tease, the piano player, who played various sections from the up-coming musical numbers. While clapping out the rhythms for the tap sequence, Renarde continually glanced offstage into the wings, his anxiety building with each new glance, until finally he called a halt to the rehearsing.

"STOP! Stop, girls! Oh, stop," the emcee shouted, quite in contrast from the congenial host that he portrayed for the evening performances. "Please, Ivory, stop playing. Everyone stop. It's very good, but it's pointless without Electra. I mean, Electra Fying is the lead performer. We need her to see if this will work. Where the hell is she?"

"Oh, Renarde," Infield cried, rushing onto the stage from the wings from which Renarde had been expecting Electra to appear for rehearsal. "I've just gotten the worst news for you. Electra called and she twisted her ankle and I don't know what we'll do.... "

"No!" Renarde gasped, aghast. "How did it happen?"

"Apparently, Electra got her costume wires crossed so she tripped and fell and now she can't even walk because it hurts like hell."

"Oh, my God!" Renarde shook his head, his eyes wide with disbelief and sympathy. "Tripping over your specialty. Every dancer's nightmare. How awful!"

"I know,… it's dreadful. And we're sold out tonight. But Dragula says you'll make it work, that you always do, and someone you will find. After all, you still have several hours before it is show time."

As Infield hurried off, shuffling out of the rehearsal, Renarde collapsed against the piano.

"A FEW HOURS! A FEW HOURS! What, is he kidding? To replace THE STAR OF THE NUMBER." Picking himself up, Renarde rushed over to an ensemble member in the first group of dancers. "Downy Soft, you'll have to take Electra's place. We have no choice."

"I can't, Renarde," Downy protested. "I have to lead the middle section."

"All right," he agreed, rushing to the next group. "April Morning, you take Electra's place."

April shook her head. "I can't possibly do it, Renarde. I have to lead the ending routine. You know that."

"All right, all right," Renarde conceded, a thread of panic entering his voice. He turned to the third group of dancers. "Cha Cha Boom! You're my last hope! Please Cha Cha!"

Cha Cha answered in the thick accent of her native Brooklyn. "And who will lead the in-between section, may I ask?"

"Oh, God, you're right. You're all right," Renarde wailed in dramatic despair, mopping at his sweating brow with the pink towel across his shoulders. "We'll never make it work. We're doomed! WE'RE DOOMED! WE HAVE NO STAR FOR TONIGHT'S
PERFORMANCE!"

As Renarde emoted dramatically, a voice spoke from the club floor in front of the stage.

"Never say never, Renarde," Dragula said, escorting a new arrival up the steps and onto the lip-shaped stage. The new "girl" was wearing a thirties wig, and was dressed in a long, very sexy shimmering evening gown. No one would have ever guessed that just a short time before this new "girl" had been riding Hair Trigger and keeping the streets safe as one of the city's finest. They stopped in front of Renarde.

"Don't I always provide a new arousal of excitement at The 'G' Spot?" Dragula asked, waving a slender finger in mock discipline at the choreographer. "I'd like you to meet our newest addition, Curtina Upp. That's Upp with two p's."

"Oh, thank God," Renarde exclaimed, grasping Dragula's hand in gratitude. "Once again, you've saved the day. But can she tap? This production number is a tap piece."

"I...I can try," Curtina answered, in a shy, light girlish voice.

"Show us what you've got," Renarde said and signaled the piano player. "Hit it, Ivory."

At Renarde's signal, as the ensemble watched expectantly, Ivory Tease played a driving tap rhythm.

Curtina hesitated, looking at Dragula nervously, and with a smile of encouragement, Dragula gestured for her to move to center stage and begin. Curtina obliged, slowly starting to tap, but her efforts were uncoordinated and amateurish at best, and she finally stopped, looking around her with embarrassment.

Bug-eyed with disbelief, Renarde took several quick shots from his inhaler, looked from the other dancers to Dragula and Curtina and started to protest. However, with the lift of a hand, Dragula stopped Renarde, and crossed to the piano.

"Ivory," Dragula said in a knowing voice, Renarde straining sideways to hear the words being uttered by The "G" Spot owner. "Could you play something that sounds like horse hooves?"

Renarde, eyebrows a-fly and head twisting back and forth from ensemble to Dragula, looked on in disbelief, but Dragula gave a gentle nod to Ivory, and the pianist began to play a slow musical clip-clop, clip-clop. Center stage, Curtina's feet slowly began to tap, her feet moving in a staccato blur as she tapped out a show-stopping routine.

"See, she just needs a little clip-clop to start her off, and she's fine."

"But why the horsy-hoof sounds?" Renarde wondered, squinting toward Curtina.

Dragula leaned in and spoke in a quiet whisper. "She's got a Hair Trigger."

"Don't we all," Renarde replied, with a head wobble of self-amusement. "All right, I suppose I can think of something to put in to get her started, but we still may have a problem. The whole number depends on the lead-in torch song, which means we need a triple threat. Can Curtina sing?"

Dragula smiled. "Listen."

Curtina took a step forward on the stage. Using plenty of diaphragmatic breath support and an open throat, just as she had been taught at the vocal lessons she took for so many years during her off-duty hours, Curtina sang with the sweetest feminine voice she could muster.

♫"Diiiiiiiiiiiiiiiiiiiiiiiick!"

Renarde swooned, took another shot of his inhaler, and looked from his dancers, who nodded adoringly, back to Curtina.

117

"That was the sweetest 'dick' I've ever heard," Renarde sighed.

"I'll leave you in Renarde's capable hands, Curtina," Dragula said, turning to go.

Curtina hurried after the departing "G" Spot star, speaking in an intent and unsure whisper. "But are you sure I can do this?"

Dragula took her young convert by the shoulders.

"Listen to me, Curtina. You've waited your whole life for this. This is your chance! And you can do it! I know it! You've got just a few hours. Listen to everything Renarde tells you, then dance and sing like you've never sung and danced before. And remember this, Curtina Upp." Dragula turned Curtina to face the club room, her hand stretched out toward the darkness before them. "You may be going out there a little nervous and unaccustomed to this new way of dressing, but you're going to come back a star!"

Curtina twittered with excitement and anticipation as Dragula exited, blowing Curtina a kiss. Renarde grabbed the new girl's arm, hurrying her to center stage, and clapped orders to everyone.

"Places, everyone. Let's try this. And for heaven's sake, concentrate! We only have a few hours. Curtina, just follow my lead. All right, Ivory, hit it!"

EIGHTEEN

SISTER TIME

Peter was with his orchids when Rachael came into the glass-enclosed greenhouse that he had built off the south side of the house where the location would allow his floral creations to receive the maximum in natural lighting and heat from the sun.

"Your text said you needed to talk to me?"

Peter crossed to meet his sister. "Yes, Rachael. Thank you for coming."

"How are you doing? Physically, I mean. Are the bruises you suffered during that horrible incident healing?"

"I'm much better, thanks. Thank God it turned out the way it did. And thank God you were there with me when it happened." Peter gestured to the two empty chairs in the corner of the room. The chairs were surrounded by orchids. "Here, let's sit."

"These flowers are truly magnificent," Rachael said, taking in the beauty of the blossoming orchids around them as she sat across from her brother. "You really do have the magic touch when it comes to orchids."

"I do my best," Peter replied quietly. "They're like my children, in a way, I guess. The beings I've raised who give me comfort when I come here…when I lock myself away from the outside world. I…I've been thinking a lot about what you said, you know…about how I lock myself away from others out of fear of being hurt…."

Rachael reached forward, taking her brother's hand. "Peter, I shouldn't have said those things. I have no right to say what I said about you and Harry."

119

"Actually, Harry and I are no longer together," Peter said, absentmindedly and tenderly caressing the folds of a nearby orchid when Rachael released his hand. "I've known the relationship wasn't working for some time. I just wasn't sure how to go about ending it. But I'm glad it did end before it became bitter and nasty. I'm actually indebted to you. You sort of helped force the issue. And you have every right to tell me how you feel, Rachael…"

"Peter, I…."

Peter raised his hand to interrupt Rachael responding. "No, you were right. That's one of the things you helped me realize. I've been very selfish and self-centered, and…I'm sorry. Not only did you do everything you could for me after Mother died, …but you have never stopped trying to watch out for me. The other night being a perfect example. You were so brave, not showing a moment's hesitation about defending me. I know you love me and I guess it's the job of those who love us to help us face the truth. So, let me say right now that I love you, Rachael, and I appreciate your support. And thank you for making me take a long, hard look at my behavior. I'm going to try to change, Rachael. To be less defensive and more open to the people around me. In fact, I've already started. In an encounter with a recent tormentor, rather than going after him, I tried turning the other cheek, as they say, and talking to him."

"And how did it turn out?"

Peter sighed, both frowning and smiling simultaneously. "I'm not quite sure, actually. It turned out to be a surprisingly unusual experience. We'll see. But the important thing is I want you to know I'm trying to change…."

Rachael's eyes glistened, a look of pleasure entering her expression. "I don't know what to say, Peter...."

Peter smiled. "You don't have to say anything. I'm just happy I finally got the message. Although, before you start congratulating yourself too much, you should be aware you're not totally right about everything. I make no apologies for being Dragula, Rach. It means much more to me than just hollow applause." Rachael started to make an apologetic reply, but again, Peter stopped her. "I know...I know you were speaking out of frustration, but you have to understand how much I love the pleasure I get from performing and what it means to me. I love the attention Dragula brings to me because...for a few brief moments in this life filled with all its hatred and prejudice...like we saw the other night...when I'm Dragula, I can finally feel free. Being Dragula allows me to experience moments of pure joy...to finally have some happiness...because...life...has been very hard for me...."

"I know that, Peter...."

"No,...please. Let me finish. You may think you know, but, Rachael, you cannot know, will never know, what it's like because you've never lived with the torment of knowing you were born into the wrong kind of body. You've never felt the humiliation of being a child who is not like all the others. You just don't understand."

Rachael leaned closer to her brother, her eyes clouding with emotion. "Then help me to understand, Peter. Because I want to. Don't you see? You're my brother, and I want to understand. I have never questioned your life choices, Peter. Not once. Whatever direction your lifestyle has taken. Don't you know that?"

"I do know that, Rachael," Peter said. "I'm sorry I said otherwise... and I will always love you for that."

"Then talk to me. Tell me the things I don't know. Don't you see that I'll support you no matter what? Talk to me. Help me understand."

After meeting his sister's gaze for several long moments, Peter rose and crossed to a metal bench, surrounded by a stunning array of lavender orchids that stood along both sides of a bay window. Next to the bench was a carved oak end table. Its beige lace doily covered the top of the end table and centered on the small rectangular tabletop was a tattered Bible. Peter sat down on the cushioned seat, patting the open space beside him.

"All right," he said. "Come, sit with me among the beautiful, innocent children I have brought into this world, and I'll try to explain."

And Rachael did.

They sat for a long time like that, surrounded by the incredible living floral wonder that her brother had created. And, their paper-thin delicate petals quivering attentively, the orchids around them listened, wondering what was taking place in their perfect world of shimmering warmth, water, light, and beauty. Wondering if these two sitting among them talking was something that would turn out to be bad or good.

And, as promised, Peter talked to his sister as he had never done before. He spoke tentatively at first, finding it hard to express old memories that normally only surfaced to reveal themselves in the world of his dreams...and nightmares. But slowly, as he reached deeper and deeper within for long-buried experiences… somehow… something very, very far inside him opened like the delicate petals of one of his exquisite flowers and, in a torrent of long buried memories, the words came rushing out of him.

John Arthur Long

Sometimes the words were hard to understand for he was sobbing in long, agonizing, emotion-wracked releases of inner pain. When that happened, Rachael took him in her arms and rocked him, crying with him until, at last, he was comforted enough to go on.

And as Rachael listened, she saw that he was right. Though she could hear the words, and try to comprehend what the experience must have been like, she could never really know his pain or the cruelty that the world exacted on someone born to such an existence.

But in the end, she did understand what growing up must have been like for her brother, and how he had come to deal with it. And what she understood was that the brother she held sobbing in her arms was someone who had taken what life had given him, and rather than sink into bitterness, he had found a way to work through the pain of his torment.

And in the end, after much talking and crying and sharing, Peter learned to understand something also. He understood that no matter how much you may be afraid to open up to those who love you for fear they won't understand, honesty and the truth of sharing prove to be pretty good things after all.

And to show Rachael what he had learned, and that he was sorry for the isolation he had forced upon their relationship, he reached for the thing that meant more to him than anything else in the world: his mother's Bible. With his mother's preserved orchid carefully nestled within the thin pages, he gathered up the Bible from the end table next to them, and placed it in Rachael's hands.

But Rachael shook her head, and through her tears, she took his hands within her own so that they held the Bible together, smiling through their tears that fell on the ancient text. They stayed that way for a long

123

time, hugging each other, sharing the Bible in their combined hands, savoring the comfort of a healed relationship.

And from their perfect world, the fragile orchids looked down on the brother and sister in each other's arms, and if they had been capable, they would have smiled at what they saw, for now they too understood. There had been no need for concern about this human element that sat in the midst of their world. There was nothing bad about it at all. It was good.

Finally breaking from hugging his sister, Peter wiped at his tears and looked at Rachael sheepishly.

"And there's one more thing I haven't told you, I'm afraid. Something that's bringing me more inner peace and happiness than ever playing Dragula could provide. I see now that I should have told you long before this, but if there was ever a perfect time, I guess this is it and I want to share it with you."

"Peter, you don't have to say anymore," Rachael protested, wiping at her own eyes. "Really...."

"Oh, yes I do because soon there will be no hiding this one," Peter insisted. "Everyone is going to know, and I want you to know before that happens. I've been in transition for a while now, and the process is almost complete."

"What do you mean?"

Peter took his sister's hand, speaking softly and straightforwardly. "I mean from now on...you should call me Patricia."

Rachael's free hand went to her open mouth as she comprehended her brother's words and, squealing with joy, she wrapped her arms around her new sister in glee, her eyes filling with tears once more.

"OH, MY GOD! Oh, my God. REALLY?" The sibling beside her smiled, nodding with pleasure at Rachael's reaction to the news. "THAT'S WONDERFUL! I AM SO HAPPY FOR YOU!"

Peter, suddenly feeling an opening of freedom...suddenly feeling free to be the woman he had chosen to become, allowed the being within him to emerge, and he became more feminine as the seconds ticked by, transitioning with physical spontaneity into Patricia as they cried in happiness together.

"You won't think it strange, having a sister instead of a brother?"

"NO, silly," came Rachael's unwavering answer. "I love you! And if this is what you need, what you want...WHAT YOU ARE, I AM OVERJOYED WITH HAPPINESS FOR YOU. So, tell me everything." She paused only a moment, grinning in acknowledgement. "Sister to sister! Oh, my God! I have a sister! All right. You said you've been in transition. Now, how far along are you in the process? And what can I do to help?"

"Pretty far along, actually...."

A hand went to the throat of Rachael's sibling, eyes widening with the realization that the voice that answered was no longer Peter's. It did not have Dragula's seductive quality, but it was feminine, none-the-less. It was almost as if, as the physical remnants of Peter slowly receded with each passing moment, free at last, Patricia was emerging to fill the void and was answering in a voice of soft, caring femininity.

"I've been taking the hormones and prescriptions for some time now. And therapy. Lots and lots of therapy. That's ongoing and will continue for as long as needed. And...." There was a short pause, but only for a moment, as the voice of Patricia rushed on. "And...that time that you wondered about...when I went away for all those weeks, I...I had the operation...down there."

Rachael's mouth opened and her hand went to it, stopping the sound of surprise. "Wow!" she finally uttered. "And how did that go....?

"All right, I guess," Patricia answered, frowning, looking away, and then back again. "Strange. There's no denying that. But, all right. The healing has been smooth. But it is strange! No more using the male urinals, that's for sure," she added, with a short laugh to try to ease the difficulty of what she was explaining. "It's something I've been a little freaked out about and need to keep discussing in therapy, but it's okay. Because, I...I'm really feeling very good about the whole process. Because I have finally become who I really am."

"Well...Patricia," Rachael said, smiling through her tears. "I am here for you! Whenever you need to talk. And I mean that. Anywhere. Anytime. I'm here."

"Good to hear," Patricia answered, standing. "Because...I've decided. Tonight's the night! I'm coming out of the closet tonight at The 'G' Spot and announcing the change to everyone." She took her sister's hand, holding her gaze. "And it would mean everything to me if you were there when I made the announcement."

"I'd be honored to be there with you,..,Patricia," Rachael answered, standing and hugging her sister, the two crying again and laughing through their tears.

"Great," Patricia said, pulling back and shaking her head in amusement as she realized that there was one more surprise in store for Rachael waiting at The "G" Spot. "And we'd better get going because I've set up a new entertainer and I knows she's very nervous about going on, so I want to be there to support her. I…think you'll recognize her when she comes on stage."

"Really, I know her? Who is it?"

"You'll have to wait and see," Patricia said, grinning. "I wouldn't want to spoil the surprise when Renarde calls, 'CURTAIN UP!'"

NINETEEN

THE CLIMAX AT THE "G" SPOT...LITERALLY

The "G" Spot was swollen to capacity, and throbbing with excitement. Word had circulated throughout the club that the opening act was going to be something special. Regulars insisted that something was definitely different.

First of all, rather than being backstage, the star, Dragula, was sitting at a reserved front table, chatting and laughing with those who sat nearby, ready to take in the opening. And...the sister was seated at Dragula's table, the two getting along better than anyone could remember, if you could believe it. Not only that, rumor also had it that Renarde was not even going to do his introductory patter. The show was going to go right into the opening number with some new "girl" that Dragula had discovered, and this was going to be her "coming out." In fact, the ubiquitous "they" said that this one was really something special, making it a new "G" Spot star not to be missed.

A raucous happiness best described the atmosphere that permeated the club. Customers were moving from table to table, drinking gaily, laughing at anything and everything. They were dressed to kill, and everyone could already tell it was going to be another great night, proving once again the adage that had become a sort of club slogan: If you needed to get off, there was no better place for it than The "G" Spot.

Finally, the club atmosphere darkened, those standing hurriedly found their seats by way of the soft glow of the phallic candles in the center of each table, and the theatrical lights came up on a smoky stage. A gauzy curtain stretched across the front of the stage below the high center vibrating glow of the red "G" Spot lips, multi-colored lights shimmering against the transparent thin material. And as a bright stage light ignited behind the curtain, Ivory Tease, wearing a tight dress, sides slit up to her ample thighs, could be seen seated behind a baby grand which, rather than in its usual Dickey Chick position at the side of the stage, was positioned more center stage in the hot flesh-colored spotlight. And standing seductively next to Ivory's piano, the new girl could be seen in silhouette and…wait…was that a costumed horse-figure lying beside her within the circle of light?

With titters and gasps, the audience leaned forward, taking in as much of the new girl as they could see behind the shifting lights of the transparent front curtain. They strained to see everything from the top of her wavy thirties brunette wig, down over the satin gown that hugged her curvaceous body, and on down to the tip of her high-heeled pumps, and gave each other glistening smiles of approval, loving the promising tease of more to come when the curtain was lifted. It certainly seemed she had the looks! And, oh my God…then there was the feminized costume horse lying next to her, legs tucked back daintily. Its lavishly braided tail and mane could just be seen, as could its huge eyelashes on its forward-tilted horsehead and the red lipstick shaping its enormous lips. Hilaaarrious! This was going to be something!

As Renarde's French-accented voice spoke in the darkness, the costume horse whinnied, gracefully came to a standing position and began to tap with its front hooves. Right on cue, the figure of the new girl moved sensuously against the flank of the costume horse, matching its movement with a sexy tap-tap-tap of her high-heeled shoes.

"Welcome!" Renarde said in the darkness. "Please give a warm moist hand for our newest addition to The 'G' Spot, who with her beautifully-maned horse companion, Hair Trigger, calls out in song to crime stoppers everywhere to be on the lookout for a mounted patrolman named Lacy Dick, who it would be a crime for her to stop loving! We give you Curtaina Upp, that's Upp with the two Ps! CURTAIN UP!"

Well, talk about fulfilling an audience's wildest expectations before the opening number even began! At the announcement of the new entertainer's name and "Hair Trigger" companion, the customers who filled The "G" Spot went wild, their applause heavy and long. At the front table, Rachael laughed gleefully with Dragula, as if at some secret joke between them, and applauded wildly toward the new performer on stage as the gauze curtain slowly lifted.

Curtina Upp waited, her expression in a sort of innocent pout, until the club settled once again into relative quiet, and then she ran her tongue along her lips, moistening them, and began to sing in a low, breathy blues voice:

♫"When I'm feelin' blue, and my heart, my heart is sick…
That's when I need him, I need him quick.

When my head's getting heavy, and the air's getting thick,
I've just got to have my Lacy Dick.

So I say, 'Diiiiick,' I say, 'Dick, will you come?'

Cause I know… Diiiiick…will make the bad times run away.

Yes, he comes every time. Yes, he comes every day.

Just when I think he won't, he says,
'The Dick is on the way…'"

And on the dimly-lit stage behind Curtina Upp, clustered in small groupings around stand-up period mikes, the other "girls" sang in unison. Her arm around the swaying costume horse, Curtina Upp's sensuous voice sang on:

♫ "He's a hero for sure. And quick with his gun.

Armed with handcuffs and pepper,

He's got them on the run.

But at the end of the shift, he holds onto that night stick.

Calling all cars, be on the lookout for Lacy Dick.

And I'll say, 'Dick,' I'll say, 'Dick, are you far?

'Cause, Dick, I know it's oh so hard…to be alone.'"

In the audience, the smiles said it all. They were loving every second of this latest "G" Spot performance.

And then, just when everything was so right, everything suddenly went wrong.

"STOP!" echoed the shout of a masculine voice that sliced through the darkened atmosphere of The "G" Spot like a knife.

"OH, DICK! OOOHHHH!"

"I SAID STOP THIS SINFUL AND DISGUSTING EXCUSE FOR ENTERTAINMENT, AND STOP IT IS WHAT YOU WILL DO!"

Striding through the audience that filled the darkened clubroom, oblivious to the unbelieving, gaping customers around him, marched a very determined Reverend Bobby Swagger, his assistant Tammy Twingle by his side. At the entrance of the club, a determined Cousin Juicy had intercepted Infield and held the struggling bouncer against the back wall.

"I'm sorry," Infield cried, fighting to free himself from where Juicy held him. "I was watching the number, and they took me by surprise. I even dropped my balls."

Onstage, Ivory grabbed Curtina's hand, rushing with her and the costume horse to the Dickey Chicks combo area. The ensemble remained in small groups at the back of the stage waiting to see what was going to happen as Swagger and Tammy Twingle came up the steps toward them, stopping front and center, and turning to face the room.

Swagger glared into the audience where Dragula sat.

"Come up on stage, Dragula," Swagger instructed in the rich bass tones of his best revivalist voice. "It is time!"

With a strong twisting turn, Infield broke from Cousin Juicy's grasp, scooped up the fallen balls from the floor in front of them and rushed forward, shaking his balls at Swagger. "What do you think you're doing...you, you, you fly in the ointment?"

Swagger smiled confidently. "As I pointed out to Dragula when we first met, things are not always as they seem. Which is precisely why I am here. It is time for Dragula to face who and what she really is."

Infield turned to those around him. "Someone call the police!"

Rachael suddenly stood. "No, wait, Infield, please." She looked down to the table where Dragula sat. "Why don't we let Dragula decide what she wants?

The picture of control, Dragula smiled up at Rachael. "Thank you for that, Rachael. Thank you for understanding."

"I do," Rachael answered, placing a hand on Dragula's shoulder. "I want you to know that."

Dragula stood and embraced Rachael. Several nearby patrons teared-up when brother and sister embraced, and dabbed at their mascara-laden eyes while, after sitting Rachael in the chair she had occupied, Dragula turned and moved confidently up the stairs onto the lip-shaped "G" Spot stage, and crossed to the center.

"Let it be, Inny," Dragula said with authority to the hovering bouncer, gesturing for him to back away. "The Reverend here is right. It is time.

Time we settled this once and for all. Let's see what the good Reverend wants."

A determined Infield refused to yield, furiously squeezing his balls as he glared at Swagger until Dragula spoke comfortingly to him once more.

"Easy, Inny. Just relax, all right? I know how you must feel, but do it for me. Everything's going to be fine." Ever the faithful servant, Infield shook his balls in Swagger's face threateningly, and then, with a nod to Dragula, retreated slowly back to his position at the entrance.

"And the rest of you, sit down and relax," Dragula instructed the anxious patrons who filled the room. "Some of you told me you were looking forward to something unusual tonight. Well, it looks like you've gotten your wish. Just sit back and enjoy the show. This is between Reverend Swagger and Dragula."

With nervous laughter, the crowd settled back into their chairs. Amazingly, Dragula didn't seem to be the least bit nervous. If that were the case, why should they be? Encouraged, several lifted their drink glasses, motioning for refills. If one didn't need a Multiple Orgasm at a time like this, when did one?

"Who knows?" Dragula continued, turning her attention exclusively to the man on stage with her. "Perhaps we can use this opportunity to help clarify some of Reverend Swagger's thinking."

"I'm the one who'll do the clarifying here," was Swagger's quick reply. "And don't try any of that slippery sweet talk on me this time because I'm not going to fall for it."

Dragula smiled. "As I tried to explain to you the last time we met, I am committed to honesty and will answer you with the truth as I know it. I give you my word."

"Exactly what are you, Dragula? A transvespire, as the club program claims? I doubt it. I think that's just so much show biz. Well, what then? This is the question that must be answered! What exactly are you and what kind of sinful activity does The 'G' Spot promote and endorse. Let's find out, shall we? First, let's look at your reflection."

Swagger looked offstage and called, "BITCHES, NOW, IF YOU PLEASE!"

To the audible gasps and murmurs and pointing from the audience, the Three Bitches suddenly rushed on stage from the wings. Each held a large mirror in front of her as the Bitches bumped into each other, bitching with utterances of, "I'm over here, you're over there, bitch,…I am not, I'm here, you're over there,…stop bitching and get over there…I'm not sure where I am…what a bitch," while Swagger waited irritably until they finally found their assigned positions on the outer edge of the stage. Once the Bitches stopped moving, stage lights picked up the mirrors, reflecting piercing beams in all directions.

"You say you know who and what you are, Dragula. Fine!" Swagger said, striding around the stage, his chest puffed out. "Why don't you tell us! I've even provided the mirrors so that you can see all sides of yourself. Come on, say it! Take a long, hard look and tell us. Tell us what you are. What are you? Are you a man?   OR ARE YOU JUST A FREAK WHO PREYS ON ALL THE INNOCENT, GOD-LOVING NORMAL PEOPLE IN THE WORLD?"

And, suddenly, there they were again. Echoes of the horrible voices of the past, this time showing their faces in the present through the bigoted personage of the Right Reverend Bobby Swagger.

And that was when the realization came to Dragula that they would always be there in some hateful bigoted form and the truth was that there was ultimately not one single thing that she could do about it. Yet, surprisingly, with this new realization, a strange relief swept over her because she suddenly discovered something else that was just as earth-shaking.

It didn't matter.

Yes, the cries of prejudice would always be there to ridicule those who chose a different lifestyle with all its implicit feelings and ways of being, but it did not matter. IT WAS THE BIGOT'S PROBLEM.

"I am what I am, Swagger," Dragula reiterated, matter-of-factly, finding there was little else to say. "And I must be true to what I am. I make no apologies for it."

"Well, I'm afraid that answer is not quite good enough, Dragula. Not by a long shot. There's just too much at stake!"

"TOO MUCH AT STAKE?" Dragula shouted, a rage filling her being for the first time. "I'll tell you what's at stake. NO LESS THAN EVERYTHING! Being true to who and what we are. That's what's at stake! When there's no way but your way, Reverend Swagger...that is when you've gone too far. You shout, you rant, you swagger, telling everyone what they should be and do. Well, I say your way is the deluded way, praised by narrow-minded bigots just like you!"

"NOOOO!" Swagger raged in response. "A man's a man; he's not a woman. It's been that way since Adam and Eve. Your way is the devil's way. It breeds sin and harm, as well it should. You still don't see it, do you! Well, you're going to! I promise you that because I'm here to stop you. To stop you for good! At last, you're going to come head to head with exactly what you've become because you must face reality! You must see the evil of your idolization! See the distortion of what you have become!"

Distracted by the two combatants at the center of the stage, no one had noticed when Cousin Juicy had pushed Timber Lake aside at the drum set. At Swagger's signal, a grinning Cousin Juicy brought the drum set alive with a loud drum roll.

"BRING IN MA DADDY!" Swagger roared, his God-inspired voice breaking into song: ♫ "BRING IN MA DADDY! I'LL NO LONGER SPAR. HERE IS MA DADDY! THE EXAGGERATION…THE ABOMINATION…SEXUAL DEVIATION…OF WHAT YOU ARE!"

From the rear of the stage, Tailgate came ushering in the enormous hermaphrodite puppet of Ma Daddy.

As the lights ignited the gleaming statuesque quality of what they saw, The "G" Spot patrons' mouths opened wide, the shock so enormous no sound escaped from them at all.

The huge puppet, Ma Daddy, was costumed in exaggerated characteristics of both male and female. It had a thick facial beard as well as large, protruding lips covered with glaring red lipstick and thick, long curling eyelashes above bulging lined eyes behind horn-rimmed glasses. The buff overly-muscled body was composed of enormous breasts protruding from a pink tank top and there was gigantic "male" padding around the genital area covered with tight jeans. On the feet were red lady's pumps with stiletto heels. And as it crossed the stage, the movement of the hermaphrodite puppet was accomplished by control sticks attached to the arms, rear torso and legs that Tailgate used to manipulate Ma Daddy's movement.

Swagger's voice rose to a fevered pitch as the Bitches shifted the mirrors to create reflections. And suddenly, enormous duplicates of Ma Daddy were everywhere, huge moving, grotesque hermaphrodite images,

John Arthur Long

bouncing and shifting in the light, covering The "G" Spot from every angle.

"FACE YOUR PERVERTED DISTORTION, SINNER!" screamed Reverend Swagger. "COME FACE TO FACE WITH YOUR SICKNESS! REPENT, DRAGULA! DO YOU AT LAST SEE THE ENORMITY OF YOUR SICKNESS? NOW DO YOU SEE THE DANGER? WE MUST STOP THE PLAGUE YOU HAVE CREATED. RENOUNCE THE SINS OF YOUR ACTIONS, DRAGULA! NOW, AS YOU FACE MA DADDY, THE SYMBOLIC HORROR OF YOUR DISTORTION, WE MUST STOP THE MONSTROSITY CALLED DRAGULA! YOU MUST STOP DRAGULA!"

It was dramatic, there was no getting around that. But, it was also nothing more than theater, and Dragula was an old hand at showbiz. Without saying a word, she crossed to the side of the stage, reached out to a metal box on the wall, opened the cover, and flicked a switch.

All the lights inside the club came on full.

The effect was so startling that everyone on stage stopped moving, blinking at the brightness, and just like that, suddenly, there was no more theatrical illusion. They were all just standing around in a fully-lighted room with a stage at one end of it, staring at an enormous, gangly, oversized costumed wooden puppet. Ma Daddy, indeed!

"Before you criticize, look to yourself, Reverend," Dragula said quietly, bringing the fever pitch that Swagger had created down to a level that could be dealt with, as she crossed back to the center of the stage. "The distortion is yours. And it is the distortion of narrow-mindedness and bigotry. That is the plague of which you speak. This may not be your way, but it's our way, our way to grab a few moments of fun and happiness. And how dare you try to take it from us. Well, we have

137

no intention of letting that happen. What we do hurts no one, and...WE'VE SUFFERED ENOUGH!" Dragula raised her arms, turning to those before her. "Let's put it to those around us: WHAT DO YOU THINK OF MA DADDY? DO YOU HATE THE HERMAPHRODITE...OR DO YOU LOOOVVVEEE ITTT?"

"WE LOVE IT," the ensemble surrounding Dragula cheered.

"And it is perfect for The 'G' Spot where it is oh so, hot, hot, hot," Renarde shouted. "Can we keep it?"

"Don't you see, Swagger," Dragula continued. "You may not agree, but why must you try to stop it? We're not hurting you or anyone else. We're just having fun!"

"BECAUSE IT'S WRONG, THAT'S WHY," Swagger cried.

"No, you're wrong," Dragula answered forcefully. "Ask these people. I have never forced anyone. I merely allowed people to do what they wanted to do."

From the ensemble surrounding Dragula and Swagger, Curtina Upp suddenly stepped forward.

"Dragula's right," Curtina said defiantly. "I just got here, and I love it. We don't need no stinking mirrors to see who we are. And I don't need no Lacy Dick to rescue me and I don't need you either, Swagger." Curtina's voice suddenly dropped to a forceful male police officer's pitch as she removed the wig from her head. "I know the law and I know we're not breaking any. We're just grabbing our own moment in showbiz to put on a show, and I love it!" With a flourish, Curtina replaced her wig, and then sang out in a loud soprano voice to punctuate her statement: ♫ "DIIIIIICCCCKKKKK!"

Taking advantage of the shifting situation, Dragula signaled to those around her, who grabbed the mirrors before the bitches holding them could protest.

"That's right," said Renarde indignantly, stepping forward as the mirrors disappeared within the ensemble. "Who do you think you are, coming here to The 'G' Spot where it is oh so, hot, hot, hot, and telling us what to do, and how to act? We like what we do, and we do what we like, and we like who we are."

"Yeah," echoed the ensemble, stepping forward as one. "We like who we are!"

"And we like Dragula!" Renarde said.

"Hey, we only did it for the money," said the Bitches, suddenly stepping forward, and pulling off their wigs to prove a point. "We love being transvestites too."

"Oh my God," Cousin Juicy said to Tailgate. "The Bitches are transvestites!"

Tailgate shrugged. "What can I tell you, Cousin Juicy. Life's a bitch."

"Of course we're transvestites," Bitch One added. "Transvestites can be bitches too, you know."

"You got that right, girl," Renarde agreed with a head wobble, and a grin to Tailgate.

"It can't be," moaned Swagger, still reeling from the disclosure of the three he had thought were on his side. "Not the Bitches too?"

Wig in place and sexual as always, Dragula stepped from among the ensemble cast of The "G" Spot, her voice sensuously female.

"You know what they say, Reverend: Don't knock it until you've tried it." She smiled mischievously and winked to those around her.

"Say, you know what I think might help to resolve this? A little affection! How about it, girls? Why don't we show Reverend Swagger there are no hard feelings? How about a group hug?"

Loving the idea, everyone on stage nodded and started toward Swagger, the audience applauding and urging them on.

"No, get back," Swagger muttered in panic, his searching gaze finding his assistant. "Tammy, you understand how wrong this is. Tell them. Make them understand."

But to Swagger's chagrin, there was something different in Tammy Twingle's manner as she stepped forward, her look proud and courageous.

"It's not just the Bitches, Bobby...I mean, Reverend Swagger! I've been thinking and listening very carefully, and, I'm sorry, but I think these people are right."

"Ohh, you've been thinking. Please, Miss Twingle," Swagger protested, his frustration growing. "Why don't you leave the thinking to me."

Tammy shook her head with newfound determination. "NO, I WILL NOT...you...you religious chauvinist! NOT ANYMORE! I'm not just some sexual object, you know, Reverend Swagger. These people aren't hurting anyone. They're simply having a good time, just like I've said from the beginning, but you refused to listen. WELL, I AGREE WITH THEM! AND I SAY: ME TOO!"

Tailgate rushed to Tammy's side as those around her applauded and shouted support. "Good for you, Tammy! Sorry, Reverend. But I'm with Tammy. She's got the courage to stand up for what she thinks is right. Now that's my kind of woman."

"Thank you for your support, Miss Tailgate," Tammy said.

"It's just Tailgate, remember," the fortuneteller answered, putting an arm around Tammy's shoulders. "To anyone who wants to party."

Desperate to stop the tide from turning against him, Swagger rushed across the stage to where Cousin Juicy stood. "Cousin Juicy, I paid five thousand dollars of the congregation's money. You promised me this would work!"

Cousin Juicy shrugged. "What can I tell ya? Life's a game of chance. Win some, lose some...bitch!"

"NOOOOO!" Swagger screamed in rage, running toward the gangling Ma Daddy, tearing at the costume that covered its hermaphroditic frame. "NO, DON'T YOU SEE WHAT THIS...THIS...THIS THING REPRESENTS?"

Then, suddenly Swagger stopped, looking in horror from the pieces of torn costume in his hands to the exposed inner structure of the puppet.

"OH, MY GOD! WAIT! WHAT...WHAT IS THIS HORRIBLE THING MADE OF?"

Cousin Juicy leaned in, nodding knowingly as he studied the puppet. "Looks like it's make of...WOOD to me."

In despair, Swagger fell to his knees his spirit, bluster and conviction totally broken, his hands clasped toward the heavens.

"WOOD! NO, NOT WOOD! THE PROPHECY WAS TRUE! OH, LORD, WHY? WHY HAST THOU FORSAKEN ME IN MY TIME OF NEED?"

"Your God has not forsaken you," Dragula said, moving to the defeated Swagger. "Don't you see? SHE'S helped you prove what is really important in all this. The sexual orientation does not matter. And...I want to thank you."

"Thank me?" an incredulous Swagger stammered, struggling to his feet with Dragula's assistance and support.

"Yes, thank you for helping me realize that every human being is sacred. And, living a life filled with love from the heart is what really matters. That's what you've helped me see. What you've really brought us face to face with tonight is the ultimate truth: that perhaps we're all male and female. And perhaps the supreme universal religious being you speak of is also both male and female. And over our lifetimes of learning, we've all been mothers, fathers, brothers, sisters, friends, all returning again and again to learn through the human experience that it is not the duality, but the unity that is important. Perhaps exploring all of who we are no matter what that looks like is the thing that will eventually allow us all to become one."

"No," Swagger insisted, shaking his head. "This...this can't be happening! This isn't the way it is supposed to go."

Dragula smiled comfortingly. "I think you know that's not true...Bobby. I think this is exactly the way it is supposed to go. And I also think that if we're really lucky, as we explore the what and who we are, we find that special soul-mate. That special person we were meant to be with." Dragula lifted Swagger's downcast face with a hand, meeting his gaze. "What's my name?"

"What do you mean? You're Dragula."

"No," Dragula said, shaking her head and removing the wig. Immediately, those around her noticed that the hairnet the entertainer always wore beneath the wig was missing and unusually long locks and waves of auburn hair fell in place around Dragula's head , framing her face in a...well, in a feminine way. "What's my name?"

"Peter," Swagger answered softly, suddenly understanding.

142

"No," Dragula said, a radiant smile emerging within her warm expression as her voice became even more feminine. "MY NAME IS PATRICIA"

Gasps of shock and reaction to the name sounded around the interior of The "G" Spot.

"No, you're Peter," Swagger muttered.

"NOT ANYMORE," Dragula shouted proudly. "I'VE MADE THE TRANSFORMATION AND IT'S TIME! I'M COMING OUT! BOTH INSIDE AND OUT, I AM A WOMAN NOW! A WOMAN WHO AT LONG LAST HAS FINALLY BECOME WHO SHE WAS BORN TO BE AND HAS FINALLY FOUND TRUE HAPPINESS! And now, I say it loud and I say it proud! PATRICIA! BECAUSE IT IS MY NAME! I AM WOMAN! HEAR ME CRY: PATRICIA!"

Thunderous applause, whistles and shouts of joy erupted as the realization of the shocking words resounded within the club.

"You're...a...woman! You mean you've made the changes both inside...and out?" Swagger uttered meekly.

"That's right, Baby!" Patricia said, moving sensuously toward Swagger. "Inside and out! I'm all woman! Aaanndd, Bobby, do you remember when we first kissed? That charge of sensation that ran through us when we embraced. That doesn't happen with everyone. But it happened with us, didn't it?"

More gasps of surprise sounded on stage and around the club as people froze, attentions riveted to the two figures in the center of the stage. There was a long pause as Swagger stared at the person he knew as Dragula, finally finding the words that he whispered quietly to help him comprehend what he had heard.

"You're really a...woman?"

143

"Yes, Bobby! And I said I would be honest and this is the truth. I've always felt alone, Bobby. And I see what I've really been doing is searching…searching for that special person I could connect with. Someone who could make me feel truly alive. I…I've tried to deny it since the moment it happened, as I know you have, but when we kissed…." More gasps sounded from those who surrounded the two. "I…I felt something ignite between us within me that I have never felt before. You felt it too. You told me you did."

"I…thought…you were Tammy," Swagger protested weakly.

Patricia nodded. "Oh, I understand. You thought I was Tammy and that you had won. And I gloated as Dragula because I thought I had gotten revenge. But why don't we both admit what really happened. Because, Bobby, the truth is we have both won. Perhaps we've known it since we first met in front of the club, and neither of us wanted to admit it. That's why I…why you…why both of us have fought so hard against each other,… are fighting so hard against it now.

"So, let's find out, Bobby. Let's strip away the phony personas. No more swaggering Swagger. No more devil's transvestite Dragula. What difference does it make if we're male or female? Can't we just be…Patricia and Bobby? Two human beings who, to the surprise of them both, suddenly found they were drawn to each other."

"No…we can't…I can't. It's wrong."

"No," Patricia insisted. "That's the one thing I know is true, Bobby. The wonderfully unique honestly-felt attraction one person has for another. Love is not…IS NOT WRONG! But if you believe it's wrong, then prove it. Prove it to me and prove it to yourself. Prove it to everyone here.

"Kiss me," Patricia said, reaching out and taking Swagger's hand as more gasps of surprise filled the club. "It won't be the first time. God didn't strike you dead or anything when it happened before. On the contrary, you said you liked it quite a bit, if I remember correctly. So, kiss me and tell me you feel nothing. I'm giving you your chance, Bobby. Kiss me. And if you tell me you feel nothing, I swear to you, I'll take off this costume and never assume the character of Dragula again. Honesty and truth, right? You will have won!" Swagger gave the tiniest negative shake of his head, but his hand remained clasped in hers. "Come on, Bobby. Do it! Just one kiss. Prove to me I'm wrong. Then there'll be no more doubt."

In the hush of the crowded space, you could have heard a pin drop as soft multi-colored lights gently turned around the two figures who stood center stage at The "G" Spot. As if through some invisible magnetic attraction, Swagger lifted his gaze and their eyes met. And Patricia and Bobby moved together, kissing softly…tenderly…their bodies not quite touching. Then, slowly, their lips parted and they moved ever-so-slightly away from each other, gazing with unblinking intensity into each other's eyes.

TWENTY

DÉNOUMENT

♫"When you might be...up the ass....

You will change your mind real fast.

It's all right to be a transvestite.

So join the party, have some fun...

Even a bigot can be one.

It's all right to be a transvestite!"

At the conclusion of the first line of Renarde's opening ditty, the lights illuminated the stage to reveal The "G" Spot's lavender-outfitted emcee holding a mike center stage and the club's ensemble posed behind him in choir robes and holding black music folders.

Bowing, Renarde blew kisses to the audience. "Hello, again, everyone. And welcome to The 'G' Spot, where it is oh, so hot, hot, hot! What a special time it is for The 'G' Spot, because tonight we have a singer who has found the error of her ways. And she is going to pour out her soul to us with music. That's right, for the first time here at The 'G' Spot, where it is oh, so hot, hot, hot, we're going to hear...the Gospel!"

Tammy Twingle, seated at a front table with Tailgate and Cousin Juicy applauded happily. "Gospel. Oh, I love gospel. Don't you?"

Tailgate wrapped an arm around Tammy's shoulders. "I love anything you love, Sugar," she said, giving Tammy a big hug. "How would you like to have another Multiple Orgasm?"

"Would I!" Tammy said. "You bet! Talk about juicy. I don't believe I've ever had anything as enjoyable as a Multiple Orgasm. Give me another one, Tailgate."

"I'll have one also," said Cousin Juicy, turning to Tailgate. "I think you should have the Bitches work on duplicating this Multiple Orgasm formula in powder form. It would be a big hit at the Health Food Center. Much better than the Horny Toad current big seller."

Tailgate downed her own Orgasm in one big swallow, grinning dreamily. "You got it, Cousin Juicy. And make that two. I agree with Tammy here. I can always use another Orgasm."

"So, get ready to clap your hands and stomp your feet," Renarde instructed the audience from the stage. "It's time to raise the roof, and a few other things. Let's put our hands together and shout praises for the vocal talents of gospel singer, ROBERTA FLACCID!"

To the welcoming applause, Renarde gestured to center stage and moved into the wings where he rested against the newly-dressed Ma Daddy, his arm wrapped affectionately around the towering hermaphrodite's waist, and for which he had paid Tailgate and the Bitches an outrageous price. Many of those in the club's performing ensemble had tried to talk him out of paying such a sum, but Renarde would have none of it. Now that the infamous Ma Daddy had found The "G" Spot, Renarde was determined Ma Daddy was there to stay, insisting The "G" Spot was right where Ma Daddy belonged.

A spotlight hit a trio of singers on stage, and to everyone's amazement and delight, posing in the spotlight were none other than the Three Bitches.

"Look, it's the Bitches," Cousin Juicy said happily, waving toward the stage. "Hello, you cute Bitches!"

The Bitches gave Cousin Juicy a quick unison wave, and then, to the astonishment of Tailgate, the three began to sing in harmony.

The trio sang center stage with slow gospel intensity as the robed chorus hummed behind. Well, to be truthful, they weren't perfectly together and they were singing a little off pitch, this being their first time in front of an audience and all, but there were no moments of bitching interrupting their singing, and they were so cute up on stage, the audience loved it.

"Amazing," Tailgate muttered, enjoying a fresh Orgasm and leaning over to Cousin Juicy. "They just needed an audience. God, if I'd known that, I could have stopped the bitching years ago."

Then, amid half-hushed gasps and discrete pointing from onlookers, Roberta Flaccid, a newly transformed Bobby Swagger, on the arm of the one-and-only Dragula, stepped into a hot spotlight, Dragula singing gleefully as they crossed to center stage.

♫ "You know she's walking like a lady.

And she's taking it for a whirl.

Oh, yes, she's dressing up and stepping out…

She's letting things unfurl.

Just see her strutting on the runway,

with her hair all bobbed and curled.

Oh, yes, she's walking tall…

She's got it all.

It's fun to be a girl."

Well, to put it kindly, Roberta Flaccid was certainly not the most attractive of transvestites, and various patrons commented so in the audience, leaning over and whispering sotto voce to one another. She was certainly nothing like the trio of cute Bitches who introduced her in song, or regulars like Downy Soft, Electra Fying, April Morning, and Cha Cha Boom. In fact, to be brutally honest, from where they sat,

Roberta Flaccid was probably the ugliest rendition of a transvestite any of them had ever laid eyes on.

First of all, look at the way the gospel choir robe hung on her! Sure it was a robe, but make it sexy, girl. It bulged in all the wrong places. See, the idea was to create a bosom, not a puffed out chest with broad shoulders that made you look like a football linebacker. Ohh, and that wig. What could she have been thinking? Bangs! Paaleeeaaase!

Then there were the shoes. Flats, no less. How the hell do you show off the curving taper of a calf with flats on your feet? Not to mention the fact that flats do a grand total of nothing in the way of lifting your ass so it will be noticed. And was she even wearing pantyhose under that robe? God, let's hope so. But if she were, flesh color was the wroooong choice! Black tights only with those legs, girl. Anything to hide the stubble on those pillars that seemed to scream, "Shave me next time before you take me into public." One couldn't even imagine what the bikini line must look like around the thong, if there even were a thong somewhere in the nether regions of the robe.

However, she was a first-timer, and they were willing to make excuses. But, really now, would you look at that face! Unplucked eyebrows. And, use a # 2 liner, sweetheart, not a crayon. Eyelashes that had to be right out of a Halloween costume package. Round circles of rouge at the top of the cheekbones. Fine, if you're a clown…but this The "G" Spot, not the circus. Feather the rouge, sweetheart… feather it. And was that a shadow of whiskers across the cheeks? Oh, God, someone have a private chat with her, paleeaaassse! Cardinal Rule # 1: Never let them see the whiskers. And those nails. Who couldn't tell they were straight out of a stick-on deluxe five-pack? With all that, what could the perfume choice possibly be: Eau De La Slut?

149

Ohhh, all right, maybe it wasn't as bad as all that. Perhaps they were being a tad catty. But could you blame them? After all, look what Roberta Flaccid had put Dragula through in her previous incarnation.

But THEN, just when everything was all horrifically tense, suddenly, there had been Dragula's announcement that she had transitioned into a complete woman!

Oh My God! PATRICIA! Talk about being true to yourself. Was there ever a better example? It was enough to take your breath away. What courage! What honesty! No empty platitudes from this one! She didn't just preach, "Be true to yourself." She did it! What a shining beacon for them all to follow!

And then, to top it all off, then there was that KISS! What a moment! What a moment at The "G" Spot, like none other! Talk about surprises and reversals. OMG! And there was no denying the attraction between them. Whoooaa! The way they had kissed so tenderly that first time, center stage for all to see. Some of those watching, mouths agape, had even teared up at the tenderness of the moment. And then, the next kiss after that first one. Zowwweeee! In front of everyone, no less! And on and on until it was almost "get a room" time. Some of the viewers even had to grab a Multiple Orgasm just to get themselves calmed down.

So, of course, it was almost a given that Dragula would put the pun-intended "Roberta Flaccid" on stage to perform after that. And, you had to hand it to Dragula. What a quintessential model of turning the other cheek for all of them to follow. However, someone was going to have to clue Roberta in that, when you did turn the other cheek, you should rub in the powder so it blends to smoothness to accent the cheekbone.

Then, as those in the audience looked her up and down with judgmental tsks and frowns, Roberta Flaccid started to sing. And there was not another catty comment to be heard! The entire audience sat in a state of complete rapture as Roberta sang...gospel! Amazing! Really! Roberta sang with an undeniable burst of gospel emotions, throwing in spiritual ad libs and everything as the ensemble hummed behind her in musical support:

♫ "I used to walk...to walk...the straight and the narrow...

I was a bigot and uptight.

I thought the only way was my way.

I didn't know my wrong from right.

But thanks to everyone, and the wonder of the night,

I found a brand new way of being,

and it feels so awfully right.

Ohh, thaaaanks to Dragula...

I learned, I learned to change my mind real fast.

Yeeeeeeeeeeesss, thanks toooo Draaaaaaaaaguuuuulaaaaaa,

I learned to...sashay with...some class!"

In the corner by the stage, the Dickey Chicks kicked the beat into high gear, and the robed ensemble began to move, clapping and dancing, their voices raised in exaltation.

Dragula spun on stage, dancing with exuberance as the ensemble clapped to the driving beat. The "G" Spot star strutted to Roberta Flaccid and removed her choir robe to reveal Roberta in full drag, the queen of the number. As they danced in the fever of religious gyrations, the ensemble members stripped off their own choir robes, revealing glittering outfits. They flung their robes into the wings and raised their hands to the heavens, waving them in praises of glory. And everyone, yes, EVERYONE delivered gospel in full-out movement and song that rocked

The "G" Spot from the LGBTQIA flag covering the back wall,

spreading throughout the house of the foot-stomping, hand-clapping appreciative patrons, and on to the quivering red-lipped entrance where an ecstatic Infield squeezed his balls as he danced with joy:

♫ "BECAUSE... I'M (SHE'S)...WALKING LIKE A LADY,
AND SHE'S TAKING IT FOR A WHIRL.

OH, YES, SHE'S DRESSING UP AND STEPPING OUT.

SHE'S LETTING THINGS UNFURL

OH, YES, SHE'S WALKING LIKE A LADY,
AND IT FEELS SO AWFULLY RIGHT!

OH, YES, SHE'S WALKING TALL, AND SHOWING OFF...
FOR EVERYONE IN SIGHT.

OH, YES, SHE'S ALL DOLLED-UP FROM HEAD TO TOE...
AND STEPPING OUT TONIGHT.

AND SHE'S WALKING LIKE A LADY...

SHE HAS BECOME A TRANS...VES...TITE.

OH, YES, SHE'S WALKING LIKE A LADY,
AND IT FEELS SO AWFULLY RIGHT.

OH, YES SHE'S WALKING LIKE A LADY.

SHE HAS BECOME A TRANS...VES...TITE!

SHE HAS BECOME...A...TRANS...VES...TITE!"

*   *   *

www.ingramcontent.com/pod-product-compliance
Lightning Source LLC
Chambersburg PA
CBHW020340260626
47156CB00004B/1621